SELECTED POEMS

by the same author

The Collected Poems of Louis MacNeice

The Dark Tower

The Agamemnon of Aeschylus
(Translation)

LOUIS MACNEICE

Selected Poems

Selected
and introduced by
W. H. AUDEN

FABER AND FABER
London · Boston

First published in this edition 1964
by Faber and Faber Limited
3 Queen Square London W.C.1
Reprinted 1968, 1972, 1977, 1979 and 1981
Printed in Great Britain by
Whitstable Litho Limited
Whitstable Kent
All rights reserved

ISBN 0 571 06089 7

Contents

The poems in this book are presented in the order of their publication, with the exception of the earliest, where the order is that adopted in Louis MacNeice's *Collected Poems* (1949), and the translations which are placed together at the end.

Introduction

The only selection from a poet's whole production which can or should have any authority with the public is the one made by himself. He alone can see the poems from the inside and evaluate them in terms of the kinds of poetry he is trying to write. In his foreword to a selection he made in 1959, Louis MacNeice wrote:

> 'These are not, I assume, my eighty-five best poems — nor, even though I like them, the eighty-five which I like best. I have excluded some which, *of their kind*, seem better than some I have let in. . . . My main object has been to illustrate diffcrent phases *and* different kinds of my work.'

The other kind of selection which, though without authority, is legitimate, is the one which each reader, once he is familiar with the whole range of the poet's work, makes for himself solely on the basis of his own personal taste, and that is all this selection is. As a fellow poet of the same generation and a personal friend, it would be both dishonest and impudent of me to play the school-master-critic and select poems, not because I like them, but because of their possible significance to a literary historian. I have, for instance, included nothing from *Autumn Sequel* or *Ten Burnt Offerings*. Posterity may judge me a fool, but it seems to me that, in the early nineteen-fifties, Louis MacNeice struck a bad patch — a misfortune which can befall any poet and often does. I would not call the poems from this period bad — like everything he wrote, they are beautifully carpentered — but I do find them a bit dull. Luckily for him and for me, this period did not last long, and his last three volumes contain, in my opinion, his finest work. Needless to say, the omission of a poem from this selection does not necessarily imply that I do not like it. A selection has no right to compete on the market with the Collected Poems, as mine certainly would, were I to include everything I admire.

Again, it is not for me, as a contemporary and a friend, to attempt a serious critical evaluation of Louis MacNeice's poetry. That task I must leave to a younger generation, confident that a just judgment will be a favourable one, and that his reputation will steadily increase with the years.

W. H. AUDEN

An Eclogue for Christmas

A. I meet you in an evil time.
B.   The evil bells
   Put out of our heads, I think, the thought of everything
      else.
A. The jaded calendar revolves,
   Its nuts need oil, carbon chokes the valves,
   The excess sugar of a diabetic culture
   Rotting the nerve of life and literature;
   Therefore when we bring out the old tinsel and frills
   To announce that Christ is born among the barbarous
      hills
   I turn to you whom a morose routine
   Saves from the mad vertigo of being what has been.
B. Analogue of me, you are wrong to turn to me,
   My country will not yield you any sanctuary,
   There is no pinpoint in any of the ordnance maps
   To save you when your towns and town-bred thoughts
      collapse,
   It is better to die *in situ* as I shall,
   One place is as bad as another. Go back where your instincts
      call
   And listen to the crying of the town-cats and the taxis again,
   Or wind your gramophone and eavesdrop on great men.
A. Jazz-weary of years of drums and Hawaiian guitar,
   Pivoting on the parquet I seem to have moved far
   From bombs and mud and gas, have stuttered on my feet
   Clinched to the streamlined and butter-smooth trulls of the
      élite,
   The lights irritating and gyrating and rotating in gauze —
   Pomade-dazzle, a slick beauty of gewgaws —
   I who was Harlequin in the childhood of the century,
   Posed by Picasso beside an endless opaque sea,
   Have seen myself sifted and splintered in broken facets,
   Tentative pencillings, endless liabilities, no assets,

Abstractions scalpelled with a palette-knife
Without reference to this particular life.
And so it has gone on; I have not been allowed to be
Myself in flesh or face, but abstracting and dissecting me
They have made of me pure form, a symbol or a pastiche,
Stylised profile, anything but soul and flesh:
And that is why I turn this jaded music on
To forswear thought and become an automaton.

B. There are in the country also of whom I am afraid —
Men who put beer into a belly that is dead,
Women in the forties with terrier and setter who whistle and
    swank
Over down and plough and Roman road and daisied
    bank,
Half-conscious that these barriers over which they stride
Are nothing to the barbed wire that has grown round their
    pride.

A. And two there are, as I drive in the city, who suddenly
    perturb —
The one sirening me to draw up by the kerb
The other, as I lean back, my right leg stretched creating
    speed,
Making me catch and stamp, the brakes shrieking, pull up
    dead:
She wears silk stockings taunting the winter wind,
He carries a white stick to mark that he is blind.

B. In the country they are still hunting, in the heavy shires
Greyness is on the fields and sunset like a line of pyres
Of barbarous heroes smoulders through the ancient air
Hazed with factory dust and, orange opposite, the moon's
    glare,
Goggling yokel-stubborn through the iron trees,
Jeers at the end of us, our bland ancestral ease;
We shall go down like palaeolithic man
Before some new Ice Age or Genghiz Khan.

A. It is time for some new coinage, people have got so old,
Hacked and handled and shiny from pocketing they have
    made bold

To think that each is himself through these accidents, being
   blind
To the fact that they are merely the counters of an unknown
   Mind.
B. A Mind that does not think, if such a thing can be,
   Mechanical Reason, capricious Identity.
   That I could be able to face this domination nor flinch —
A. The tin toys of the hawker move on the pavement inch by
   inch
   Not knowing that they are wound up; it is better to be so
   Than to be, like us, wound up and while running down to
   know —
B. But everywhere the pretence of individuality recurs —
A. Old faces frosted with powder and choked in furs.
B. The jutlipped farmer gazing over the humpbacked wall.
A. The commercial traveller joking in the urinal.
B. I think things draw to an end, the soil is stale.
A. And over-elaboration will nothing now avail,
   The street is up again, gas, electricity or drains,
   Ever-changing conveniences, nothing comfortable remains
   Un-improved, as flagging Rome improved villa and sewer
   (A sound-proof library and a stable temperature).
   Our street is up, red lights sullenly mark
   The long trench of pipes, iron guts in the dark,
   And not till the Goths again come swarming down the hill
   Will cease the clangour of the pneumatic drill.
   But yet there is beauty narcotic and deciduous
   In this vast organism grown out of us:
   On all the traffic-islands stand white globes like moons,
   The city's haze is clouded amber that purrs and croons,
   And tilting by the noble curve bus after tall bus comes
   With an osculation of yellow light, with a glory like
      chrysanthemums.
B. The country gentry cannot change, they will die in their
   shoes
   From angry circumstance and moral self-abuse,
   Dying with a paltry fizzle they will prove their lives to be
   An ever-diluted drug, a spiritual tautology.

13

They cannot live once their idols are turned out,
None of them can endure, for how could they, possibly,
    without
The flotsam of private property, pekinese and polyanthus,
The good things which in the end turn to poison and pus,
Without the bandy chairs and the sugar in the silver tongs
And the inter-ripple and resonance of years of dinner-gongs?
Or if they could find no more that cumulative proof
In the rain dripping off the conservatory roof?
What will happen when the only sanction the country-
    dweller has —

A. What will happen to us, planked and panelled with jazz?
Who go the theatre where a black man dances like an eel,
Where pink thighs flash like the spokes of a wheel, where we
    feel
That we know in advance all the jogtrot and the cake-walk
    jokes,
All the bumfun and the gags of the comedians in boaters and
    toques,
All the tricks of the virtuosos who invert the usual —

B. What will happen to us when the State takes down the manor
    wall,
When there is no more private shooting or fishing, when the
    trees are all cut down,
When faces are all dials and cannot smile or frown —

A. What will happen when the sniggering machine-guns in the
    hands of the young men
Are trained on every flat and club and beauty parlour and
    Father's den?
What will happen when our civilisation like a long pent
    balloon —

B. What will happen will happen; the whore and the buffoon
Will come off best; no dreamers, they cannot lose their
    dream
And are at least likely to be reinstated in the new régime.
But one thing is not likely —

A.   Do not gloat over yourself
Do not be your own vulture, high on some mountain shelf

Huddle the pitiless abstractions bald about the neck
Who will descend when you crumple in the plains a wreck.
Over the randy of the theatre and cinema I hear songs
Unlike anything —

B.   The lady of the house poises the silver tongs
And picks a lump of sugar, 'ne plus ultra' she says
'I cannot do otherwise, even to prolong my days' —

A. I cannot do otherwise either, tonight I will book my seat —

B. I will walk about the farm-yard which is replete
As with the smell of dung so with memories —

A. I will gorge myself to satiety with the oddities
Of every artiste, official or amateur,
Who has pleased me in my rôle of hero-worshipper
Who has pleased me in my rôle of individual man —

B. Let us lie once more, say 'What we think, we can'
The old idealist lie —

A.   And for me before I die
Let me go the round of the garish glare —

B.   And on the bare and high
Places of England, the Wiltshire Downs and the Long Mynd
Let the balls of my feet bounce on the turf, my face burn in
    the wind
My eyelashes stinging in the wind, and the sheep like grey
    stones
Humble my human pretensions —

A.   Let the saxophones and the xylophones
And the cult of every technical excellence, the miles of canvas
    in the galleries
And the canvas of the rich man's yacht snapping and tacking
    on the seas
And the perfection of a grilled steak —

B.   Let all these so ephemeral things
Be somehow permanent like the swallow's tangent wings:
Goodbye to you, this day remember is Christmas, this morn
They say, interpret it your own way, Christ is born.

Eclogue by a Five-barred Gate

(Death and two Shepherds)

D. There is no way here, shepherds, read the wooden sign,
    Your road is a blind road, all this land is mine.

1. But your fields, mister, would do well for our sheep.

2. They could shelter from the sun where the low hills dip.

D. I have sheep of my own, see them over there.

1. There seems no nater in 'em, they look half dead.

2. They be no South Downs, they look so thin and bare.

D. More than half, shepherds, they are more than half dead.
    But where are your own flocks you have been so talking of?

1. Right here at our elbow —

2.   Or they *was* so just now.

D. That's right, shepherd, they was so just now.
    Your sheep are gone, they can't speak for you,
    I must have your credentials, sing me who you are.

1. I am a shepherd of the Theocritean breed,
    Been pasturing my songs, man and boy, this thirty year —

2. And for me too my pedigree acceptances
    Have multiplied beside the approved streams.

D. This won't do, shepherds, life is not like that,
    And when it comes to death I may say he is not like that.
    Have you never thought of Death?

1.   Only off and on,
    Thanatos in Greek, the accent proparoxytone —

2. That's not what he means, he means the thing behind the
        word
    Same as took Alice White the time her had her third —

D. Cut out for once the dialect and the pedantry,
    I thought a shepherd was a poet —

1.   On his flute —

2.   On his oat —

D. I thought he was a poet and could quote the prices
    Of significant living and decent dying, could lay the rails level
        on the sleepers
    To carry the powerful train of abstruse thought —

16

1. What an idea!
2.   But certainly poets are sleepers,
   The sleeping beauty behind the many-coloured hedge —
D. All you do is burke the other and terrible beauty, all you do is
       hedge
   And shirk the inevitable issue, all you do
   Is shear your sheep to stop your ears.
   Poetry you think is only the surface vanity,
   The painted nails, the hips narrowed by fashion,
   The hooks and eyes of words; but it is not that only,
   And it is not only the curer sitting by the wayside,
   Phials on his trestle, his palms grown thin as wafers
   With blessing the anonymous heads;
   And poetry is not only the bridging of two-banked rivers.
2. Who ever heard of a river without a further bank?
D. You two never heard of it.
   Tell me now, I have heard the cuckoo, there is tar on your
       shoes,
   I surmise that spring is here —
2.   Spring be here truly,
   On Bank Holiday I wore canvas shoes,
   Could feel the earth —
D.   And that being so, tell me
   Don't you ever feel old?
2.   There's a question now.
1. It is a question we all have to answer,
   And I may say that when I smell the beans or hear the
       thrush
   I feel a wave intensely bitter-sweet and topped with silver —
D. There you go again, your self-congratulation
   Blunts all edges, insulates with wool,
   No spark of reality possible.
   Can't you peel off for even a moment that conscious face?
   All time is not your tear-off jotter, you cannot afford to
       scribble
   So many so false answers.
   This escapism of yours is blasphemy,
   An immortal cannot blaspheme for one way or another

17

His trivialities will pattern in the end;
But for you your privilege and panic is to be mortal
And with Here and Now for your anvil
You must strike while the iron is hot —

2.   He is an old man,
That is why he talks so.

D.   Can't you understand me?
Look, I will set you a prize like any of your favourites,
Like any Tityrus or tired Damon;
Sing me, each in turn, what dream you had last night
And if either's dream rings true, to him I will open my gate.

2. Ho, here's talking.

1.   Let me collect myself.

D. Collect yourself in time for if you win my prize —

2. I'm going to sing first, I had a rare dream.

1. Your dream is nothing —

D.   The more nothing the better.

1. My dream will word well —

2.   But not wear well —

D. No dreams wear at all as dreams.
Water appears tower only while in well —
All from the same comes, the same drums sound
In the pulsation of all the bulging suns,
And no clock whatever, while winding or running down,
Makes any difference to time however the long-legged
     weights
Straggle down the cottage wall or the child grows leggy
     too —

1. I do not like your talking.

2.   It gives giddiness
Like the thrumming of the telephone wires in an east wind
With the bellyache and headache and nausea.

D. It is not my nature to talk, so sing your pieces
And I will try, what is repugnant too, to listen.

1. Last night as the bearded lips of sleep
Closed with the slightest sigh on me and I sank through the
     blue soft caves
Picked with light delicate as the chink of coins

18

Or stream on the pebbles I was caught by hands
And a face was swung in my eyes like a lantern
Swinging on the neck of a snake.
And that face I knew to be God and I woke,
And now I come to look at yours, stranger,
There is something in the lines of it —

D.   Your dream, shepherd,
Is good enough of its kind. Now let us hear yours.

2.   Well, I dreamt it was a hot day, the territorials
Were out on melting asphalt under the howitzers,
The brass music bounced on the houses. Come
I heard cry as it were a water-nymph, come and fulfil me
And I sped floating, my feet plashing in the tops of the wheat
But my eyes were blind,
I found her with my hands lying on the drying hay,
Wet heat in the deeps of the hay as my hand delved,
And I possessed her, gross and good like the hay,
And she went and my eyes regained sight and the sky was full
     of ladders
Angels ascending and descending with a shine like
     mackerel —
Now I come to tell it it sounds nonsense.

D.   Thank you, gentlemen, these two dreams are good,
Better than your daytime madrigals.
If you really wish I will give you both the prize,
But take another look at my land before you choose it.

1.   It looks colder now.

2.   The sheep have not moved.

1.   I have a fancy there is no loving there
Even among sheep.

D.   They do not breed or couple.

1 & 2. And what about us, shall we enjoy it there?

D. *Enjoy what where ?*

2.   Why, life in your land.

D. I will open this gate that you may see for yourselves.

1.   You go first.

2.   Well, you come too.

1 & 2. We will go together to these pastures new . . .

19

D. So; they are gone; life in my land . . .
There is no life as there is no land.
They are gone and I am alone
With a gate the façade of a mirage.

Elephant Trunk

Descending out of the grey
Clouds elephant trunk
Twitches away
Hat;
THAT
Was *not* what I expected,
A
Misdirected
Joke it seemed to me;
'What about a levitation?' I had said,
Preening head for halo,
All alert, combed, sanctified,
I thank Thee, Lord, I am not like other men
WHEN
Descending out of the grey
Clouds elephant trunk. . . .

(and so *ad nauseam.*)

River in Spate

The river falls and over the walls the coffins of cold funerals
Slide deep and sleep there in the close tomb of the pool,
And yellow waters lave the grave and pebbles pave its mortuary
And the river horses vault and plunge with their assault and
      battery,
And helter-skelter the coffins come and the drums beat and the
      waters flow,
And the panther horses lift their hooves and paw and shift and
      draw the bier,
The corpses blink in the rush of the river, and out of the water
      their chins they tip
And quaff the gush and lip the draught and crook their heads and
      crow,
Drowned and drunk with the cataract that carries them and
      buries them
And silts them over and covers them and lilts and chuckles over
      their bones;
The organ-tones that the winds raise will never pierce the water
      ways,
So all they will hear is the fall of hooves and the distant shake of
      harness,
And the beat of the bells on the horses' heads and the undertaker's
      laughter,
And the murmur that will lose its strength and blur at length to
      quietness,
And afterwards the minute heard descending, never ending
      heard,
And then the minute after and the minute after the minute after.

Happy Families

The room is all a stupid quietness,
Cajoled only by the fire's caress;
We loll severally about and sit
Severally and do our business severally,
For there's a little bit for everybody;
But that's not all there is to it.

Crusted in sandstone, while the wooden clock
Places two doctor fingers on his mouth,
We seem fossils in rock,
Or leaves turned mummies in drouth,
And garnered into a mouldy shrubbery corner
Where the wind has done with us. When we are old
The gardener will use us for leaf-mould.

Dutifully sitting on chair, lying on sofa,
Standing on hearth-rug, here we are again,
John caught the bus, Joshua caught the train,
And I took a taxi, so we all got somewhere;
No one deserted, no one was a loafer,
Nobody disgraced us, luckily for us
No one put his foot in it or missed the bus.

But the wind is a beggar and always
Raps at front door, back door, side door;
In spite of the neat placard that says
'No Hawkers Here' he knocks the more.
He blows loose paper into petulance
And ruffles the brazier's fiery hair; and once
He caught me suddenly surreptitiously
And heft me out of my shell. We'll pass that over
And forget about it and quietly sit
Knitting close, sitting close under cover.

Snuff out the candle, for the cap, I think,
Seems to fit, excellently fit.
Te saluto — in a fraction, half a wink —
But that's not all there is to it.

Spring Sunshine

In a between world, a world of amber,
The old cat on the sand-warm window-sill
Sleeps on the verge of nullity.

Spring sunshine has a quality
Transcending rooks and the hammering
Of those who hang new pictures,
Asking if it is worth it
To clamour and caw, to add stick to stick for ever.

If it is worth while really
To colonise any more the already populous
Tree of knowledge, to portion and reportion
Bits of broken knowledge brittle and dead,
Whether it would not be better
To hide one's head in the warm sand of sleep
And be embalmed without hustle or bother.

The rooks bicker heckle bargain always
And market carts lumber —
Let me in the calm of the all-humouring sun
Also indulge my humour
And bury myself beyond creaks and cawings
In a below world, a bottom world of amber.

Circe

'. . . vitreamque Circen'

Something of glass about her, of dead water,
Chills and holds us,
Far more fatal than painted flesh or the lodestone of live hair
This despair of crystal brilliance.
Narcissus' error
Enfolds and kills us —
Dazed with gazing on that unfertile beauty
Which is our own heart's thought.
Fled away to the beasts
One cannot stop thinking; Timon
Kept on finding gold.
In parrot-ridden forest or barren coast
A more importunate voice than bird or wave
Escutcheoned on the air with ice letters
Seeks and, of course, finds us
(Of course, being our echo).

Be brave, my ego, look into your glass
And realise that that never-to-be-touched
Vision is your mistress.

Spring Voices

The small householder now comes out warily
Afraid of the barrage of sun that shouts cheerily,
Spring is massing forces, birds wink in air,
The battlemented chestnuts volley green fire,
The pigeons banking on the wind, the hoots of cars,
Stir him to run wild, gamble on horses, buy cigars;
Joy lies before him to be ladled and lapped from his hand —
Only that behind him, in the shade of his villa, memories stand
Breathing on his neck and muttering that all this has happened
      before,
Keep the wind out, cast no clout, try no unwarranted jaunts
      untried before,
But let the spring slide by nor think to board its car
For it rides West to where the tangles of scrap-iron are;
Do not walk, these voices say, between the bucking clouds alone
Or you may loiter into a suddenly howling crater, or fall, jerked
      back, garrotted by the sun.

Snow

The room was suddenly rich and the great bay-window was
Spawning snow and pink roses against it
Soundlessly collateral and incompatible:
World is suddener than we fancy it.

World is crazier and more of it than we think,
Incorrigibly plural. I peel and portion
A tangerine and spit the pips and feel
The drunkenness of things being various.

And the fire flames with a bubbling sound for world
Is more spiteful and gay than one supposes —
On the tongue on the eyes on the ears in the palms of one's
    hands —
There is more than glass between the snow and the huge roses.

Sunday Morning

Down the road someone is practising scales,
The notes like little fishes vanish with a wink of tails,
Man's heart expands to tinker with his car
For this is Sunday morning, Fate's great bazaar;
Regard these means as ends, concentrate on this Now,
And you may grow to music or drive beyond Hindhead anyhow,
Take corners on two wheels until you go so fast
That you can clutch a fringe or two of the windy past,
That you can abstract this day and make it to the week of time
A small eternity, a sonnet self-contained in rhyme.

But listen, up the road, something gulps, the church spire
Opens its eight bells out, skulls' mouths which will not tire
To tell how there is no music or movement which secures
Escape from the weekday time. Which deadens and endures.

Birmingham

Smoke from the train-gulf hid by hoardings blunders upward,
    the brakes of cars
Pipe as the policeman pivoting round raises his flat hand, bars
With his figure of a monolith Pharaoh the queue of fidgety
    machines
(Chromium dogs on the bonnet, faces behind the triplex screens).
Behind him the streets run away between the proud glass of shops,
Cubical scent-bottles artificial legs arctic foxes and electric mops,
But beyond this centre the slumward vista thins like a diagram:
There, unvisited, are Vulcan's forges who doesn't care a tinker's
    damn.

Splayed outwards through the suburbs houses, houses for rest
Seducingly rigged by the builder, half-timbered houses with lips
    pressed
So tightly and eyes staring at the traffic through bleary haws
And only a six-inch grip of the racing earth in their concrete
    claws;
In these houses men as in a dream pursue the Platonic Forms
With wireless and cairn terriers and gadgets approximating to the
    fickle norms
And endeavour to find God and score one over the neighbour
By climbing tentatively upward on jerry-built beauty and sweated
    labour.

The lunch hour: the shops empty, shopgirls' faces relax
Diaphanous as green glass, empty as old almanacs
As incoherent with ticketed gewgaws tiered behind their heads
As the Burne-Jones windows in St. Philip's broken by crawling
    leads;
Insipid colour, patches of emotion, Saturday thrills
(This theatre is sprayed with 'June') — the gutter take our old
    playbills,
Next week-end it is likely in the heart's funfair we shall pull
Strong enough on the handle to get back our money; or at any rate
    it is possible.

On shining lines the trams like vast sarcophagi move
Into the sky, plum after sunset, merging to duck's egg, barred with
    mauve
Zeppelin clouds, and Pentecost-like the cars' headlights bud
Out from sideroads and the traffic signals, crême-de-menthe or
    bull's blood,
Tell one to stop, the engine gently breathing, or to go on
To where like black pipes of organs in the frayed and fading zone
Of the West the factory chimneys on sullen sentry will all night
    wait
To call, in the harsh morning, sleep-stupid faces through the daily
    gate.

Carrickfergus

I was born in Belfast between the mountain and the gantries
  To the hooting of lost sirens and the clang of trams:
Thence to Smoky Carrick in County Antrim
  Where the bottle-neck harbour collects the mud which jams

The little boats beneath the Norman castle,
  The pier shining with lumps of crystal salt;
The Scotch Quarter was a line of residential houses
  But the Irish Quarter was a slum for the blind and halt.

The brook ran yellow from the factory stinking of chlorine,
  The yarn-mill called its funeral cry at noon;
Our lights looked over the lough to the lights of Bangor
  Under the peacock aura of a drowning moon.

The Norman walled this town against the country
  To stop his ears to the yelping of his slave
And built a church in the form of a cross but denoting
  The list of Christ on the cross in the angle of the nave.

I was the rector's son, born to the anglican order,
  Banned for ever from the candles of the Irish poor;
The Chichesters knelt in marble at the end of a transept
  With ruffs about their necks, their portion sure.

The war came and a huge camp of soldiers
  Grew from the ground in sight of our house with long
Dummies hanging from gibbets for bayonet practice
  And the sentry's challenge echoing all day long;

A Yorkshire terrier ran in and out by the gate-lodge
  Barred to civilians, yapping as if taking affront:
Marching at ease and singing 'Who Killed Cock Robin?'
  The troops went out by the lodge and off to the Front.

The steamer was camouflaged that took me to England —
    Sweat and khaki in the Carlisle train;
I thought that the war would last for ever and sugar
    Be always rationed and that never again

Would the weekly papers not have photos of sandbags
    And my governess not make bandages from moss
And people not have maps above the fireplace
    With flags on pins moving across and across —

Across the hawthorn hedge the noise of bugles,
    Flares across the night,
Somewhere on the lough was a prison ship for Germans,
    A cage across their sight.

I went to school in Dorset, the world of parents
    Contracted into a puppet world of sons
Far from the mill girls, the smell of porter, the salt-mines
    And the soldiers with their guns.

The Sunlight on the Garden

The sunlight on the garden
Hardens and grows cold,
We cannot cage the minute
Within its nets of gold,
When all is told
We cannot beg for pardon.

Our freedom as free lances
Advances towards its end;
The earth compels, upon it
Sonnets and birds descend;
And soon, my friend,
We shall have no time for dances.

The sky was good for flying
Defying the church bells
And every evil iron
Siren and what it tells:
The earth compels,
We are dying, Egypt, dying

And not expecting pardon,
Hardened in heart anew,
But glad to have sat under
Thunder and rain with you,
And grateful too
For sunlight on the garden.

Chess

At the penultimate move, their saga nearly sung,
They have worked so hard to prove what lads they were when
    young,
Have looked up every word in order to be able to say
The gay address unheard when they were dumb and gay.
Your Castle to King's Fourth under your practised hand !
What is the practice worth, so few being left to stand?
Better the raw levies jostling in the square
Than two old men in a crevice sniping at empty air ;
The veterans on the pavement puff their cheeks and blow
The music of enslavement that echoes back 'I told you so' ;
The chapped hands fumble flutes, the tattered posters cry
Their craving for recruits who have not had time to die.
While our armies differ they move and feel the sun,
The victor is a cypher once the war is won.
Choose your gambit, vary the tactics of your game,
You move in a closed ambit that always ends the same.

Eclogue from Iceland

Scene: *The Arnarvatn Heath. Craven, Ryan and the ghost of Grettir. Voice from Europe.*

R.   This is the place, Craven, the end of our way;
        Hobble the horses, we have had a long day.

C.   The night is closing like a fist
        And the long glacier lost in mist.

R.   Few folk come this time of year.
        What are those limping steps I hear?

C.   Look, there he is coming now.
        We shall have some company anyhow.

R.   It must be the mist — he looks so big;
        He is walking lame in the left leg.

G.   Good evening, strangers. So you too
        Are on the run? I welcome you.
        I am Grettir Asmundson,
        Dead many years. My day is done.
        But you whose day is sputtering yet
        I forget. . . . What did I say?
        We forget when we are dead
        The blue and red, the grey and gay.
        Your day spits with a damp wick,
        Will fizzle out if you're not quick.
        Men have been chilled to death who kissed
        Wives of mist, forgetting their own
        Kind who live out of the wind.
        My memory goes, goes —— Tell me
        Are there men now whose compass leads
        Them always down forbidden roads?
        Greedy young men who take their pick
        Of what they want but have no luck;
        Who leap the toothed and dour crevasse
        Of death on a sardonic phrase?
        You with crowsfeet round your eyes
        How are things where you come from?

C.   Things are bad. There is no room

	To move at ease, to stretch or breed —
G.	And you with the burglar's underlip
	In your land do things stand well?
R.	In my land nothing stands at all
	But some fly high and some lie low.
G.	Too many people. My memory will go,
	Lose itself in the hordes of modern people.
	Memory is words ; we remember what others
	Say and record of ourselves — stones with the runes.
	Too many people — sandstorm over the words.
	Is your land also an island?
	There is only hope for people who live upon islands
	Where the Lowest Common labels will not stick
	And the unpolluted hills will hold your echo.
R.	I come from an island, Ireland, a nation
	Built upon violence and morose vendettas.
	My diehard countrymen like drayhorses
	Drag their ruin behind them.
	Shooting straight in the cause of crooked thinking
	Their greed is sugared with pretence of public spirit.
	From all which I am an exile.
C.	Yes, we are exiles,
	Gad the world for comfort.
	This Easter I was in Spain before the Civil War
	Gobbling the tripper's treats, the local colour,
	Storks over Avila, the coffee-coloured waters of Ronda,
	The comedy of the bootblacks in the cafés,
	The legless beggars in the corridors of the trains,
	Dominoes on marble tables, the architecture
	Moorish mudejar churriguerresque,
	The bullfight — the banderillas like Christmas candles,
	And the scrawled hammer and sickle :
	It was all copy — impenetrable surface.
	I did not look for the sneer beneath the surface.
	Why should I trouble, an addict to oblivion
	Running away from the gods of my own hearth
	With no intention of finding gods elsewhere?
R.	And so we came to Iceland —

C.   Our latest joyride.
G.   And what have you found in Iceland?
C.   What have we found? More copy, more surface,
        Vignettes as they call them, dead flowers in an album —
        The harmoniums in the farms, the fine-bread and pan-
            cakes
        The pot of ivy trained across the window,
        Children in gumboots, girls in black berets.
R.   And dead craters and angled crags.
G.   The crags which saw me jockey doom for twenty
        Years from one cold hide-out to another;
        The last of the saga heroes
        Who had not the wisdom of Njal or the beauty of Gunnar
        I was the doomed tough, disaster kept me witty;
        Being born the surly jack, the ne'er-do-well, the loiterer
        Hard blows exalted me.
        When the man of will and muscle achieves the curule
            chair
        He turns to a bully; better is his lot as outlaw
        A wad of dried fish in his belt, a snatch of bilberries
        And riding the sullen landscape far from friends
        Through the jungle of lava, dales of frozen fancy,
        Fording the gletcher, ducking the hard hail,
        And across the easy pastures, never stopping
        To rest among the celandines and bogcotton.
        Under a curse I would see eyes in the night,
        Always had to move on; craving company
        In the end I lived on an island with two others.
        To fetch fire I swam the crinkled fjord,
        The crags were alive with ravens whose low croak
        Told my ears what filtered in my veins —
        The sense of doom. I wore it gracefully,
        The fatal clarity that would not budge
        But without false pride in martyrdom. For I,
        Joker and dressy, held no mystic's pose,
        Not wishing to die preferred the daily goods,
        The horse-fight, women's thighs, a joint of meat.
C.   But this dyspeptic age of ingrown cynics

Wakes in the morning with a coated tongue
And whets itself laboriously to labour
And wears a blasé face in the face of death.
Who risk their lives neither to fill their bellies
Nor to avenge an affront nor grab a prize
But out of bravado or to divert ennui
Driving fast cars and climbing foreign mountains.
Outside the delicatessen shop the hero
With his ribbons and his empty pinned-up sleeve
Cadges for money while with turned-up collars
His comrades blow through brass the Londonderry Air
And silken legs and swinging buttocks advertise
The sale of little cardboard flags on pins.

G.   Us too they sold
The women and the men with many sheep.
Graft and aggression, legal prevarication
Drove out the best of us,
Secured long life to only the sly and the dumb
To those who would not say what they really thought
But got their ends through pretended indifference
And through the sweat and blood of thralls and hacks
Cheating the poor men of their share of drift
The whale on Kaldbak in the starving winter.

R.   And so today at Grimsby men whose lives
Are warped in Arctic trawlers load and unload
The shining tons of fish to keep the lords
Of the market happy with cigars and cars.

C.   What is that music in the air —
Organ-music coming from far?

R.   Honeyed music — it sounds to me
Like the Wurlitzer in the Gaiety.

G.   I do not hear anything at all.

C.   Imagine the purple light on the stage

R.   The melting moment of a stinted age

C.   The pause before the film again
Bursts in a shower of golden rain.

G.   I do not hear anything at all.

C.   We shall be back there soon, to stand in queues

For entertainment and to work at desks,
To browse round counters of dead books, to pore
On picture catalogues and Soho menus,
To preen ourselves on the reinterpretation
Of the words of obsolete interpreters,
Collate delete their faded lives like texts,
Admire Flaubert, Cézanne — the tortured artists —
And leaning forward to knock out our pipes
Into the fire protest that art is good
And gives a meaning and a slant to life.

G.   The dark is falling. Soon the air
Will stare with eyes, the stubborn ghost
Who cursed me when I threw him. Must
The ban go on for ever? I,
A ghost myself, have no claim now to die.

R.   Now I hear the music again —
Strauss and roses — hear it plain.
The sweet confetti of music falls
From the high Corinthian capitals.

C.   Her head upon his shoulder lies. . . .
Blend to the marrow as the music dies.

G.   Brought up to the rough-house we took offence quickly
Were sticklers for pride, paid for it as outlaws —

C.   Like Cavalcanti whose hot blood lost him Florence

R.   Or the Wild Geese of Ireland in Mid-Europe.
Let us thank God for valour in abstraction
For those who go their own way, will not kiss
The arse of law and order nor compound
For physical comfort at the price of pride:
Soldiers of fortune, renegade artists, rebels and sharpers
Whose speech not cramped to Yea and Nay explodes
In crimson oaths like peonies, who brag
Because they prefer to taunt the mask of God,
Bid him unmask and die in the living lightning.
What is that voice maundering, meandering?

VOICE. Blues . . . blues . . . high heels and manicured hands
Always self-conscious of the vanity bag
And puritan painted lips that abnegate desire

37

And say 'we do not care' . . . 'we do not care' —
I don't care always in the air
Give my hips a shake always on the make
Always on the mend coming around the bend
Always on the dance with an eye to the main
Chance, always taking the floor again —

C. There was Tchekov,
His haemorrhages drove him out of Moscow
The life he loved, not born to it, who thought
That when the windows blurred with smoke and talk
So that no-one could see out, then conversely
The giants of frost and satans of the peasant
Could not look in, impose the evil eye.

R. There was MacKenna
Spent twenty years translating Greek philosophy
Ill and tormented, unwilling to break contract,
A brilliant talker who left
The salon for the solo flight of Mind.

G. There was Onund Treefoot
Came late and lame to Iceland, made his way
Even though the land was bad and the neighbours
  jealous.

C. There was that dancer
Who danced the War, then falling into coma
Went with hunched shoulders through the ivory gate.

R. There was Connolly
Vilified now by the gangs of Catholic Action.

G. There was Egil
Hero and miser who when dying blind
Would have thrown his money among the crowd to hear
The whole world scuffle for his hoarded gold.

C. And there were many
Whose commonsense or sense of humour or mere
Desire for self assertion won them through

R. But not to happiness. Though at intervals
They paused in sunlight for a moment's fusion
With friends or nature till the cynical wind
Blew the trees pale —

VOICE.   Blues, blues, sit back, relax
               Let your self-pity swell with the music and clutch
               Your tiny lavendered fetishes. Who cares
               If floods depopulate China? I don't care
               Always in the air sitting among the stars
               Among the electric signs among the imported wines
               Always on the spree climbing the forbidden tree
               Tossing the peel of the apple over my shoulder
               To see it form the initials of a new intrigue
G.   Runes and runes which no one could decode
R.   Wrong numbers on the 'phone — she never answered.
C.   And from the romantic grill (Spanish baroque)
               Only the eyes looked out which I see now.
G.   You see them now?
C.   But seen before as well.
G.   And many times to come, be sure of that.
R.   I know them too
               These eyes which hang in the northern mist, the brute
               Stare of stupidity and hate, the most
               Primitive and false of oracles.
C.   The eyes
               That glide like snakes behind a thousand masks —
               All human faces fit them, here or here:
               Dictator, bullying schoolboy or common lout,
               Acquisitive women, financiers, invalids,
               Are capable all of that compelling stare
               Stare which betrays the cosmic purposelessness
               The nightmare noise of the scythe upon the hone,
               Time sharpening his blade among high rocks alone.
R.   The face that fate hangs as a figurehead
               Above the truncheon or the nickelled death.
G.   I won the fall. Though cursed for it, I won.
C.   Which is why we honour you who working from
               The common premises did not end with many
               In the blind alley where the trek began.
G.   Though the open road is hard with frost and dark.
VOICE. Hot towels for the men, mud packs for the women
               Will smooth the puckered minutes of your lives.

I offer you each a private window, a view
(The leper window reveals a church of lepers).
R.   Do you believe him?
C.   I don't know.
  Do you believe him?
G.   No.
  You cannot argue with the eyes or voice;
  Argument will frustrate you till you die
  But go your own way, give the voice the lie,
  Outstare the inhuman eyes. That is the way.
  Go back to where you came from and do not keep
  Crossing the road to escape them, do not avoid the
      ambush,
  Take sly detours, but ride the pass direct.
C.   But the points of axes shine from the scrub, the odds
  Are dead against us. There are the lures of women
  Who, half alive, invite to a fuller life
  And never loving would be loved by others.
R.   Who fortify themselves in pasteboard castles
  And plant their beds with the cast-out toys of children,
  Dead pines with tinsel fruits, nursery beliefs
  And South Sea Island trinkets. Watch their years
  The permutations of lapels and gussets,
  Of stuffs — georgette or velvet or corduroy —
  Of hats and eye-veils, of shoes, lizard or suède,
  Of bracelets, milk or coral, of zip bags
  Of compacts, lipstick, eyeshade and coiffures
  All tributary to the wished ensemble
  The carriage of body that belies the soul.
C.   And there are the men who appear to be men of sense
  Good company and dependable in a crisis,
  Who yet are ready to plug you as you drink
  Like dogs who bite from fear; for fear of germs
  Putting on stamps by licking the second finger,
  For fear of opinion overtipping in bars,
  For fear of thought studying stupefaction.
  It is the world which these have made where dead
  Greek words sprout out in tin on sallow walls —

Clinic or polytechnic — a world of slums
Where any day now may see the Gadarene swine
Rush down the gullets of the London tubes
When the enemy, x or y, let loose their gas.

G. My friends, hounded like me, I tell you still
Go back to where you belong. I could have fled
To the Hebrides or Orkney, been rich and famous,
Preferred to assert my rights in my own country,
Mine which were hers for every country stands
By the sanctity of the individual will.

R. Yes, he is right,
C.   But we have not his strength
R. Could only abase ourselves before the wall
Of shouting flesh
C.   Could only offer our humble
Deaths to the unknown god, unknown but worshipped,
Whose voice calls in the sirens of destroyers.

G. Minute your gesture but it must be made —
Your hazard, your act of defiance and hymn of hate,
Hatred of hatred, assertion of human values,
Which is now your only duty.

C. Is it our only duty?
G.   Yes, my friends.
What did you say? The night falls now and I
Must beat the dales to chase my remembered acts.
Yes, my friends, it is your only duty.
And, it may be added, it is your only chance.

Eclogue between the Motherless

A.   What did you do for the holiday?
B.   I went home.
        What did you do?
A.   O, I went home for the holiday.
        Had a good time?
B.   Not bad as far as it went.
        What about you?
A.   O quite a good time on the whole —
(both) Quite a good time on the whole at home for the holiday
A.   As far as it went — In a way it went too far,
        Back to childhood, back to the backwoods mind;
        I could not stand a great deal of it, bars on the brain
        And the blinds drawn in the drawingroom not to fade the
            chair covers
B.   There were no blinds drawn in ours; my father has married
            again —
        A girl of thirty who had never had any lovers
        And wants to have everything bright
A.   That sounds worse than us.
        Our old house is just a grass-grown tumulus,
        My father sits by himself with the bossed decanter,
        The garden is going to rack, the gardener
        Only comes three days, most of our money was in linen
B.   My new stepmother is wealthy, you should see her in
            jodhpurs
        Brisking in to breakfast from a morning canter.
        I don't think he can be happy
A.   How can you tell?
        That generation is so different
B.   I suppose your sister
        Still keeps house for yours?
A.   Yes and she finds it hell.
        Nothing to do in the evenings.
B.   Talking of the evenings
        I can drop the ash on the carpet since my divorce.
        Never you marry, my boy. One marries only

Because one thinks one is lonely — and so one was
But wait till the lonely are two and no better

A.   As a matter
Of fact I've got to tell you

B.   The first half year
Is heaven come back from the nursery — swansdown
        kisses —
But after that one misses something

A.   My dear,
Don't depress me in advance; I've got to tell you —

B.   My wife was warmth, a picture and a dance,
Her body electric — silk used to crackle and her gloves
Move where she left them. How one loves the surface
But how one lacks the core — Children of course
Might make a difference

A.   Personally I find
I cannot go on any more like I was. Which is why
I took this step in the dark

B.   What step?

A.   I thought
I too might try what you

B.   Don't say that you
And after all this time

A.   Let's start from the start.
When I went home this time there was nothing to do
And so I got haunted. Like a ball of wool
That kittens have got at, all my growing up
All the disposed-of process of my past
Unravelled on the floor — One can't proceed any more
Except on a static past; when the ice-floe breaks
What's the good of walking? Talking of ice
I remembered my mother standing against the sky
And saying 'Go back in the house and change your shoes'
And I kept having dreams and kept going back in the
        house.
A sense of guilt like a scent — The day I was born
I suppose that that same hour was full of her screams

B.   You're run down

A.   Wait till you hear what I've done.
It was not only dreams; even the crockery (odd
It's not all broken by now) and the rustic seat in the
        rockery
With the bark flaked off, all kept reminding me, binding
My feet to the floating past. In the night at the lodge
A dog was barking as when I was little in the night
And I could not budge in the bed clothes. Lying alone
I felt my legs were paralysed into roots
And the same cracks in what used to be the nursery ceiling
Gave me again the feeling I was young among ikons,
Helpless at the feet of faceless family idols,
Walking the tightrope over the tiger-pit,
Running the gauntlet of inherited fears;
So after all these years I turned in the bed
And grasped the want of a wife and heard in the rain
On the gravel path the steps of all my mistresses
And wondered which was coming or was she dead
And her shoes given to the char which tapped through
        London —
The black streets mirrored with rain and stained with
        lights.
I dreamed she came while a train
Was running behind the trees (with power progressing),
Undressing deftly she slipped cool knees beside me,
The clipped hair on her neck prickled my tongue
And the whole room swung like a ship till I woke with
        the window
Jittering in its frame from the train passing the garden
Carrying its load of souls to a different distance.
And of others, isolated by associations,
I thought — the scent of syringa or always wearing
A hat of fine white straw and never known in winter —
Splinters of memory. When I was little I sorted
Bits of lustre and glass from the heap behind the henhouse;
They are all distorted now the beautiful sirens
Mutilated and mute in dream's dissection,
Hanged from pegs in the Bluebeard's closet of the brain,

44

Never again nonchalantly to open
The doors of disillusion. Whom recording
The night marked time, the dog at the lodge kept barking
And as he barked the big cave open of hell
Where all their voices were one and stuck at a point
Like a gramophone needle stuck on a notched record.
I thought 'Can I find a love beyond the family
And feed her to the bed my mother died in
Between the tallboys and the vase of honesty
On which I was born and groped my way from the cave
With a half-eaten fruit in my hand, a passport meaning
Enforced return for periods to that country?
Or will one's wife also belong to that country
And can one never find the perfect stranger?

B.   My complaint was that she stayed a stranger.
I remember her mostly in the car, stopping by the white
Moons of the petrol pumps, in a camelhair rug
Comfortable, scented and alien.

A.   That's what I want,
Someone immutably alien —
Send me a woman with haunches out of the jungle
And frost patterns for fancies,
The hard light of sun upon water in diamonds dancing
And the brute swagger of the sea; let her love be the drop
From the cliff of my dream, be the axe on the block
Be finesse of the ice on the panes of the heart
Be careless, be callous, be glass frolic of prisms
Be eyes of guns through lashes of barbed wire,
Be the gaoler's smile and all that breaks the past.

B.   Odd ideals you have; all I wanted
Was to get really close but closeness was
Only a glove on the hand, alien and veinless,
And yet her empty gloves could move

A.   My next move
Is what I've got to tell you, I picked on the only
One who would suit and wrote proposing marriage

B.   Who is she?

A.   But she can't have yet received it;

She is in India.
B.   India be damned.
What is her name?
A.   I said I cannot offer
Anything you will want
B.   Why?
A.   and I said
I know in two years' time it will make no difference.
I was hardly able to write it at the claw-foot table
Where my mother kept her diary. There I sat
Concocting a gambler's medicine; the afternoon was cool,
The ducks drew lines of white on the dull slate of the pool
And I sat writing to someone I hardly knew
And someone I shall never know well. Relying on that
I stuck up the envelope, walked down the winding drive,
All that was wanted a figurehead, passed by the lodge
Where the dog is chained and the gates, relying on my
        mood
To get it posted
B.   Who is the woman?
A.   relying
B.   Who is the woman?
A.   She is dying
B.   Dying of what?
A.   Only a year to live
B.   Forgive me asking
But
A.   Only a year and ten yards down the road
I made my goal where it has always stood
Waiting for the last
B.   You must be out of your mind;
If it were anyone else I should not mind
A.   Waiting for the last collection before dark
The pillarbox like an exclamation mark.

Elephants

Tonnage of instinctive
Wisdom in tinsel,
Trunks like questions
And legs like tree trunks

On each forehead
A buxom blonde
And round each leg
A jangle of bells,

Deep in each brain
A chart of tropic
Swamp and twilight
Of creepered curtains,

Shamble in shoddy
Finery forward
And make their salaams
To the tiers of people —

Dummies with a reflex
Muscle of laughter
When they see the mountains
Come to Mahomet . . .

Efficacy of engines,
Obstinacy of darkness.

Bagpipe Music

It's no go the merrygoround, it's no go the rickshaw,
All we want is a limousine and a ticket for the peepshow.
Their knickers are made of crêpe-de-chine, their shoes are made of
    python,
Their halls are lined with tiger rugs and their walls with heads of
    bison.

John MacDonald found a corpse, put it under the sofa,
Waited till it came to life and hit it with a poker,
Sold its eyes for souvenirs, sold its blood for whiskey,
Kept its bones for dumb-bells to use when he was fifty.

It's no go the Yogi-Man, it's no go Blavatsky,
All we want is a bank balance and a bit of skirt in a taxi.

Annie MacDougall went to milk, caught her foot in the heather,
Woke to hear a dance record playing of Old Vienna.
It's no go your maidenheads, it's no go your culture,
All we want is a Dunlop tyre and the devil mend the puncture.

The Laird o' Phelps spent Hogmanay declaring he was sober,
Counted his feet to prove the fact and found he had one foot over.
Mrs. Carmichael had her fifth, looked at the job with repulsion,
Said to the midwife 'Take it away; I'm through with over-
    production'.

It's no go the gossip column, it's no go the Ceilidh,
All we want is a mother's help and a sugar-stick for the baby.

Willie Murray cut his thumb, couldn't count the damage,
Took the hide of an Ayrshire cow and used it for a bandage.
His brother caught three hundred cran when the seas were lavish,
Threw the bleeders back in the sea and went upon the parish.

It's no go the Herring Board, it's no go the Bible,
All we want is a packet of fags when our hands are idle.

It's no go the picture palace, it's no go the stadium,
It's no go the country cot with a pot of pink geraniums,
It's no go the Government grants, it's no go the elections,
Sit on your arse for fifty years and hang your hat on a pension.

It's no go my honey love, it's no go my poppet;
Work your hands from day to day, the winds will blow the profit.
The glass is falling hour by hour, the glass will fall for ever,
But if you break the bloody glass you won't hold up the weather.

Christmas Shopping

Spending beyond their income on gifts for Christmas —
Swing doors and crowded lifts and draperied jungles —
What shall we buy for our husbands and sons
    Different from last year?

Foxes hang by their noses behind plate glass —
Scream of macaws across festoons of paper —
Only the faces on the boxes of chocolates are free
    From boredom and crowsfeet.

Sometimes a chocolate box girl escapes in the flesh,
Lightly manoeuvres the crowd, trilling with laughter;
After a couple of years her feet and her brain will
    Tire like the others.

The great windows marshal their troops for assault on the purse,
Something-and-eleven the yard, hoodwinking logic,
The eleventh hour draining the gurgling pennies
    Down to the conduits

Down to the sewers of money — rats and marshgas —
Bubbling in maundering music under the pavement;
Here go the hours of routine, the weight on our eyelids —
    Pennies on corpses'.

While over the street in the centrally heated public
Library dwindling figures with sloping shoulders
And hands in pockets, weighted in the boots like chessmen,
    Stare at the printed

Columns of ads, the quickset road to riches,
Starting at a little and temporary but once we're
Started who knows whether we shan't continue,
    Salaries rising,

Rising like a salmon against the bullnecked river,
Bound for the spawning-ground of care-free days —
Good for a fling before the golden wheels run
    Down to a standstill.

And Christ is born — The nursery glad with baubles,
Alive with light and washable paint and children's
Eyes expects as its due the accidental
    Loot of a system.

Smell of the South — oranges in silver paper,
Dates and ginger, the benison of firelight,
The blue flames dancing round the brandied raisins,
    Smiles from above them,

Hands from above them as of gods but really
These their parents, always seen from below, them-
Selves are always anxious looking across the
    Fence to the future —

Out there lies the future gathering quickly
Its blank momentum; through the tubes of London
The dead winds blow the crowds like beasts in flight from
    Fire in the forest.

The little firtrees palpitate with candles
In hundreds of chattering households where the suburb
Straggles like nervous handwriting, the margin
    Blotted with smokestacks.

Further out on the coast the lighthouse moves its
Arms of light through the fog that wads our welfare,
Moves its arms like a giant at Swedish drill whose
    Mind is a vacuum.

The Hebrides

On those islands
The west wind drops its messages of indolence,
No one hurries, the Gulf Stream warms the gnarled
Rampart of gneiss, the feet of the peasant years
Pad up and down their sentry-beat not challenging
Any comer for the password — only Death
Comes through unchallenged in his general's cape.
The houses straggle on the umber moors,
The Aladdin lamp mutters in the boarded room
Where a woman smoors the fire of fragrant peat.
No one repeats the password for it is known,
All is known before it comes to the lips —
Instinctive wisdom. Over the fancy vases
The photos with the wrinkles taken out,
The enlarged portraits of the successful sons
Who married wealth in Toronto or New York,
Console the lonely evenings of the old
Who live embanked by memories of labour
And child-bearing and scriptural commentaries.
On those islands
The boys go poaching their ancestral rights —
The Ossianic salmon who take the yellow
Tilt of the river with a magnet's purpose —
And listen breathless to the tales at the ceilidh
Among the peat-smoke and the smells of dung
That fill the felted room from the cave of the byre.
No window opens of the windows sunk like eyes
In a four-foot wall of stones casually picked
From the knuckly hills on which these houses crawl
Like black and legless beasts who breathe in their sleep
Among the piles of peat and pooks of hay —
A brave oasis in the indifferent moors.
And while the stories circulate like smoke,
The sense of life spreads out from the one-eyed house
In wider circles through the lake of night
In which articulate man has dropped a stone —

In wider circles round the black-faced sheep,
Wider and fainter till they hardly crease
The ebony heritage of the herded dead.
On those islands
The tinkers whom no decent girl will go with,
Preserve the Gaelic tunes unspoiled by contact
With the folk-fancier or the friendly tourist,
And preserve the knowledge of horse-flesh and preserve
The uncompromising empire of the rogue.
On those islands
The tethered cow grazes among the orchises
And figures in blue calico turn by hand
The ground beyond the plough, and the bus, not stopping,
Drops a parcel for the lonely household
Where men remembering stories of eviction
Are glad to have their land though mainly stones —
The honoured bones which still can hoist a body.
On those islands
There is echo of the leaping fish, the identical
Sound that cheered the chiefs at ease from slaughter;
There is echo of baying hounds of a lost breed
And echo of MacCrimmon's pipes lost in the cave;
And seals cry with the voices of the drowned.
When men go out to fish, no one must say 'Good luck'
And the confidences told in a boat at sea
Must be as if printed on the white ribbon of a wave
Withdrawn as soon as printed — so never heard.
On those islands
The black minister paints the tour of hell
While the unregenerate drink from the bottle's neck
In gulps like gauntlets thrown at the devil's head
And spread their traditional songs across the hills
Like fraying tapestries of fights and loves,
The boar-hunt and the rope let down at night —
Lost causes and lingering home-sickness.
On those islands
The fish come singing from the drunken sea,
The herring rush the gunwales and sort themselves

To cram the expectant barrels of their own accord —
Or such is the dream of the fisherman whose wet
Leggings hang on the door as he sleeps returned
From a night when miles of net were drawn up empty.
On those islands
A girl with candid eyes goes out to marry
An independent tenant of seven acres
Who goes each year to the south to work on the roads
In order to raise a rent of forty shillings,
And all the neighbours celebrate their wedding
With drink and pipes and the walls of the barn reflect
The crazy shadows of the whooping dancers.
On those islands
Where many live on the dole or on old-age pensions
And many waste with consumption and some are drowned
And some of the old stumble in the midst of sleep
Into the pot-hole hitherto shunned in dreams
Or falling from the cliff among the shrieks of gulls
Reach the bottom before they have time to wake —
Whoever dies on the islands and however
The whole of the village goes into three day mourning,
The afflicted home is honoured and the shops are shut
For on those islands
Where a few surnames cover a host of people
And the art of being a stranger with your neighbour
Has still to be imported, death is still
No lottery ticket in a public lottery —
The result to be read on the front page of a journal —
But a family matter near to the whole family.
On those islands
Where no train runs on rails and the tyrant time
Has no clock-towers to signal people to doom
With semaphore ultimatums tick by tick,
There is still peace though not for me and not
Perhaps for long — still peace on the bevel hills
For those who still can live as their fathers lived
On those islands.

from *Autumn Journal*

II

Spider, spider, twisting tight —
  But the watch is wary beneath the pillow —
I am afraid in the web of night
    When the window is fingered by the shadows of
      branches,
When the lions roar beneath the hill
  And the meter clicks and the cistern bubbles
And the gods are absent and the men are still —
  Noli me tangere, my soul is forfeit.
Some now are happy in the hive of home,
  Thigh over thigh and a light in the night nursery,
And some are hungry under the starry dome
  And some sit turning handles.
Glory to God in the Lowest, peace beneath the earth,
  Dumb and deaf at the nadir;
I wonder now whether anything is worth
  The eyelid opening and the mind recalling.
And I think of Persephone gone down to dark,
  No more a virgin, gone the garish meadow,
But why must she come back, why must the snowdrop
    mark
  That life goes on for ever?
There are nights when I am lonely and long for love
  But to-night is quintessential dark forbidding
Anyone beside or below me; only above
  Pile high the tumulus, good-bye to starlight.
Good-bye the Platonic sieve of the Carnal Man
  But good-bye also Plato's philosophising;
I have a better plan
  To hit the target straight without circumlocution.
If you can equate Being in its purest form
  With denial of all appearance,
Then let me disappear — the scent grows warm
  For pure Not-Being, Nirvana.

Only the spider spinning out his reams
    Of colourless thread says Only there are always
Interlopers, dreams,
    Who let no dead dog lie nor death be final;
Suggesting, while he spins, that to-morrow will outweigh
    To-night, that Becoming is a match for Being,
That to-morrow is also a day,
    That I must leave my bed and face the music.
As all the others do who with a grin
    Shake off sleep like a dog and hurry to desk or engine
And the fear of life goes out as they clock in
    And history is reasserted.
Spider, spider, your irony is true;
    Who am I — or I — to demand oblivion?
I must go out to-morrow as the others do
    And build the falling castle;
Which has never fallen, thanks
    Not to any formula, red tape or institution,
Not to any creeds or banks,
    But to the human animal's endless courage.
Spider, spider, spin
    Your register and let me sleep a little,
Not now in order to end but to begin
    The task begun so often.

IV

September has come and I wake
    And I think with joy how whatever, now or in future, the
        system
Nothing whatever can take
    The people away, there will always be people
For friends or for lovers though perhaps
    The conditions of love will be changed and its vices **diminished**
And affection not lapse
    To narrow possessiveness, jealousy founded on vanity.
September has come, it is *hers*
    Whose vitality leaps in the autumn,

Whose nature prefers
  Trees without leaves and a fire in the fire-place;
So I give her this month and the next
  Though the whole of my year should be hers who has rendered
    already
So many of its days intolerable or perplexed
  But so many more so happy;
Who has left a scent on my life and left my walls
  Dancing over and over with her shadow,
Whose hair is twined in all my waterfalls
  And all of London littered with remembered kisses.
So I am glad
  That life contains her with her moods and moments
More shifting and more transient than I had
  Yet thought of as being integral to beauty;
Whose mind is like the wind on a sea of wheat,
  Whose eyes are candour,
And assurance in her feet
  Like a homing pigeon never by doubt diverted.
To whom I send my thanks
  That the air has become shot silk, the streets are music,
And that the ranks
  Of men are ranks of men, no more of cyphers.
So that if now alone
  I must pursue this life, it will not be only
A drag from numbered stone to numbered stone
  But a ladder of angels, river turning tidal.
Off hand, at times hysterical, abrupt,
  You are one I always shall remember,
Whom cant can never corrupt
    Nor argument disinherit.
Frivolous, always in a hurry, forgetting the address,
  Frowning too often, taking enormous notice
Of hats and backchat — how could I assess
  The thing that makes you different?
You whom I remember glad or tired,
  Smiling in drink or scintillating anger,
Inopportunely desired

On boats, on trains, on roads when walking
Sometimes untidy, often elegant,
  So easily hurt, so readily responsive,
To whom a trifle could be an irritant
  Or could be balm and manna.
Whose words would tumble over each other and pelt
  From pure excitement,
Whose fingers curl and melt
  When you were friendly.
I shall remember you in bed with bright
  Eyes or in a café stirring coffee
Abstractedly and on your plate the white
  Smoking stub your lips had touched with crimson.
And I shall remember how your words could hurt
  Because they were so honest
And even your lies were able to assert
  Integrity of purpose.
And it is on the strength of knowing you
  I reckon generous feeling more important
Than the mere deliberating what to do
  When neither the pros nor cons affect the pulses.
And though I have suffered from your special strength
  Who never flatter for points nor fake responses
I should be proud if I could evolve at length
  An equal thrust and pattern.

IX

Now we are back to normal, now the mind is
  Back to the even tenor of the usual day
Skidding no longer across the uneasy camber
  Of the nightmare way.
We are safe though others have crashed the railings
  Over the river ravine; their wheel-tracks carve the bank
But after the event all we can do is argue
  And count the widening ripples where they sank.
October comes with rain whipping around the ankles
  In waves of white at night

And filling the raw clay trenches (the parks of London
    Are a nasty sight).
In a week I return to work, lecturing, coaching,
    As impresario of the Ancient Greeks
Who wore the chiton and lived on fish and olives
    And talked philosophy or smut in cliques;
Who believed in youth and did not gloze the unpleasant
    Consequences of age;
What is life, one said, or what is pleasant
    Once you have turned the page
Of love? The days grow worse, the dice are loaded
    Against the living man who pays in tears for breath;
Never to be born was the best, call no man happy
    This side death.
Conscious — long before Engels — of necessity
    And therein free
They plotted out their life with truism and humour
    Between the jealous heaven and the callous sea.
And Pindar sang the garland of wild olive
    And Alcibiades lived from hand to mouth
Double-crossing Athens, Persia, Sparta,
    And many died in the city of plague, and many of drouth
In Sicilian quarries, and many by the spear and arrow
    And many more who told their lies too late
Caught in the eternal factions and reactions
    Of the city-state.
And free speech shivered on the pikes of Macedonia
    And later on the swords of Rome
And Athens became a mere university city
    And the goddess born of the foam
Became the kept hetaera, heroine of Menander,
    And the philosopher narrowed his focus, confined
His efforts to putting his own soul in order
    And keeping a quiet mind.
And for a thousand years they went on talking,
    Making such apt remarks,
A race no longer of heroes but of professors
    And crooked business men and secretaries and clerks,

Who turned out dapper little elegiac verses
    On the ironies of fate, the transience of all
Affections, carefully shunning an over-statement
    But working the dying fall.
The Glory that was Greece: put it in a syllabus, grade it
    Page by page
To train the mind or even to point a moral
    For the present age:
Models of logic and lucidity, dignity, sanity,
    The golden mean between opposing ills
Though there were exceptions of course but only exceptions —
    The bloody Bacchanals on the Thracian hills.
So the humanist in his room with Jacobean panels
    Chewing his pipe and looking on a lazy quad
Chops the Ancient World to turn a sermon
    To the greater glory of God.
But I can do nothing so useful or so simple;
    These dead are dead
And when I should remember the paragons of Hellas
    I think instead
Of the crooks, the adventurers, the opportunists,
    The careless athletes and the fancy boys,
The hair-splitters, the pedants, the hard-boiled sceptics
    And the Agora and the noise
Of the demagogues and the quacks; and the women pouring
    Libations over graves
And the trimmers at Delphi and the dummies at Sparta and lastly
    I think of the slaves.
And how one can imagine oneself among them
    I do not know;
It was all so unimaginably different
    And all so long ago.

XXIV

Sleep, my body, sleep, my ghost,
    Sleep, my parents and grand-parents,

And all those I have loved most:
　One man's coffin is another's cradle.
Sleep, my past and all my sins,
　In distant snow or dried roses
Under the moon for night's cocoon will open
　When day begins.
Sleep, my fathers, in your graves
　On upland bogland under heather;
What the wind scatters the wind saves,
　A sapling springs in a new country.
Time is a country, the present moment
　A spotlight roving round the scene;
We need not chase the spotlight,
　The future is the bride of what has been.
Sleep, my fancies and my wishes,
　Sleep a little and wake strong,
The same but different and take my blessing —
　A cradle-song.
And sleep, my various and conflicting
　Selves I have so long endured,
Sleep in Asclepius' temple
　And wake cured.
And you with whom I shared an idyll
　Five years long,
Sleep beyond the Atlantic
　And wake to a glitter of dew and to bird-song.
And you whose eyes are blue, whose ways are foam,
　Sleep quiet and smiling
And do not hanker
　For a perfection which can never come.
And you whose minutes patter
　To crowd the social hours,
Curl up easy in a placid corner
　And let your thoughts close in like flowers.
And you, who work for Christ, and you, as eager
　For a better life, humanist, atheist,
And you, devoted to a cause, and you, to a family,
　Sleep and may your beliefs and zeal persist.

Sleep quietly, Marx and Freud,
  The figure-heads of our transition.
Cagney, Lombard, Bing and Garbo,
  Sleep in your world of celluloid.
Sleep now also, monk and satyr,
  Cease your wrangling for a night.
Sleep, my brain, and sleep, my senses,
  Sleep, my hunger and my spite.
Sleep, recruits to the evil army,
  Who, for so long misunderstood,
Took to the gun to kill your sorrow;
  Sleep and be damned and wake up good
While we sleep, what shall we dream?
  Of Tir nan Og or South Sea islands,
Of a land where all the milk is cream
  And all the girls are willing?
Or shall our dream be earnest of the real
  Future when we wake,
Design a home, a factory, a fortress
  Which, though with effort, we can really make?
What is it we want really?
  For what end and how?
If it is something feasible, obtainable,
  Let us dream it now,
And pray for a possible land
  Not of sleep-walkers, not of angry puppets,
But where both heart and brain can understand
  The movements of our fellows;
Where life is a choice of instruments and none
  Is debarred his natural music,
Where the waters of life are free of the ice-blockade of hunger
  And thought is free as the sun,
Where the altars of sheer power and mere profit
  Have fallen to disuse,
Where nobody sees the use
  Of buying money and blood at the cost of blood and money,
Where the individual, no longer squandered
  In self-assertion, works with the rest, endowed

With the split vision of a juggler and the quick lock of a taxi,
    Where the people are more than a crowd.
So sleep in hope of this — but only for a little;
    Your hope must wake
While the choice is yours to make,
    The mortgage not foreclosed, the offer open.
Sleep serene, avoid the backward
    Glance; go forward, dreams, and do not halt
(Behind you in the desert stands a token
    Of doubt — a pillar of salt).
Sleep, the past, and wake, the future,
    And walk out promptly through the open door;
But you, my coward doubts, may go on sleeping,
    You need not wake again — not any more.
The New Year comes with bombs, it is too late
    To dose the dead with honourable intentions:
If you have honour to spare, employ it on the living;
    The dead are dead as Nineteen-Thirty-Eight.
Sleep to the noise of running water
    To-morrow to be crossed, however deep;
This is no river of the dead or Lethe,
    To-night we sleep
On the banks of Rubicon — the die is cast;
    There will be time to audit
The accounts later, there will be sunlight later
    And the equation will come out at last.

Stylite

The saint on the pillar stands,
The pillar is alone,
He has stood so long
That he himself is stone;
Only his eyes
Range across the sand
Where no one ever comes
And the world is banned.

Then his eyes close,
He stands in his sleep,
Round his neck there comes
The conscience of a rope,
And the hangman counting
Counting to ten —
At nine he finds
He has eyes again.

The saint on the pillar stands,
The pillars are two,
A young man opposite
Stands in the blue,
A white Greek god,
Confident, with curled
Hair above the groin
And his eyes on the world.

Entirely

If we could get the hang of it entirely
    It would take too long;
All we know is the splash of words in passing
    And falling twigs of song,
And when we try to eavesdrop on the great
    Presences it is rarely
That by a stroke of luck we can appropriate
    Even a phrase entirely.

If we could find our happiness entirely
    In somebody else's arms
We should not fear the spears of the spring nor the city's
    Yammering fire alarms
But, as it is, the spears each year go through
    Our flesh and almost hourly
Bell or siren banishes the blue
    Eyes of Love entirely.

And if the world were black or white entirely
    And all the charts were plain
Instead of a mad weir of tigerish waters,
    A prism of delight and pain,
We might be surer where we wished to go
    Or again we might be merely
Bored but in brute reality there is no
    Road that is right entirely.

London Rain

The rain of London pimples
The ebony street with white
And the neon-lamps of London
Stain the canals of night
And the park becomes a jungle
In the alchemy of night.

My wishes turn to violent
Horses black as coal —
The randy mares of fancy,
The stallions of the soul —
Eager to take the fences
That fence about my soul.

Across the countless chimneys
The horses ride and across
The country to the channel
Where warning beacons toss,
To a place where God and No-God
Play at pitch and toss.

Whichever wins I am happy
For God will give me bliss
But No-God will absolve me
From all I do amiss
And I need not suffer conscience
If the world was made amiss.

Under God we can reckon
On pardon when we fall
But if we are under No-God
Nothing will matter at all,
Adultery and murder
Will count for nothing at all.

So reinforced by logic
As having nothing to lose

My lust goes riding horseback
To ravish where I choose,
To burgle all the turrets
Of beauty as I choose.

But now the rain gives over
Its dance upon the town,
Logic and lust together
Come dimly tumbling down,
And neither God nor No-God
Is either up or down.

The argument was wilful,
The alternatives untrue,
We need no metaphysics
To sanction what we do
Or to muffle us in comfort
From what we did not do.

Whether the living river
Began in bog or lake,
The world is what was given,
The world is what we make.
And we only can discover
Life in the life we make.

So let the water sizzle
Upon the gleaming slates,
There will be sunshine after
When the rain abates
And rain returning duly
When the sun abates.

My wishes now come homeward,
Their gallopings in vain,
Logic and lust are quiet
And again it starts to rain;
Falling asleep I listen
To the falling London rain.

Order to View

It was a big house, bleak;
Grass on the drive;
We had been there before
But memory, weak in front of
A blistered door, could find
Nothing alive now;
The shrubbery dripped, a crypt
Of leafmould dreams; a tarnished
Arrow over an empty stable
Shifted a little in the almost wind,

And wishes were unable
To rise; on the garden wall
The pear trees had come loose
From rotten loops; one wish,
A rainbow bubble, rose,
Faltered, broke in the dull
Air — What was the use?
The bell-pull would not pull
And the whole place, one might
Have supposed, was deadly ill:
The world was closed,

And remained closed until
A sudden angry tree
Shook itself like a setter
Flouncing out of a pond
And beyond the sombre line
Of limes a cavalcade
Of clouds rose like a shout of
Defiance. Near at hand
Somewhere in a loose-box
A horse neighed
And all the curtains flew out of
The windows; the world was open.

Flight of the Heart

Heart, my heart, what will you do?
There are five lame dogs and one deaf-mute
All of them with demands on you.

I will build myself a copper tower
With four ways out and no way in
But mine the glory, mine the power.

And what if the tower should shake and fall
With three sharp taps and one big bang?
What would you do with yourself at all?

I would go in the cellar and drink the dark
With two quick sips and one long pull,
Drunk as a lord and gay as a lark.

But what when the cellar roof caves in
With one blue flash and nine old bones?
How, my heart, will you save your skin?

I will go back where I belong
With one foot first and both eyes blind,
I will go back where I belong
In the fore-being of mankind.

Autobiography

In my childhood trees were green
And there was plenty to be seen.

Come back early or never come.

My father made the walls resound,
He wore his collar the wrong way round.

Come back early or never come.

My mother wore a yellow dress;
Gentle, gently, gentleness.

Come back early or never come.

When I was five the black dreams came;
Nothing after was quite the same.

Come back early or never come.

The dark was talking to the dead;
The lamp was dark beside my bed.

Come back early or never come.

When I woke they did not care;
Nobody, nobody was there.

Come back early or never come.

When my silent terror cried,
Nobody, nobody replied.

Come back early or never come.

I got up; the chilly sun
Saw me walk away alone.

Come back early or never come.

Evening in Connecticut

Equipoise: becalmed
Trees, a dome of kindness;
Only the scissory noise of the grasshoppers;
Only the shadows longer and longer.

The lawn a raft
In a sea of singing insects,
Sea without waves or mines or premonitions:
Life on a china cup.

But turning. The trees turn
Soon to brocaded autumn.
Fall. The fall of dynasties; the emergence
Of sleeping kings from caves —

Beard over the breastplate,
Eyes not yet in focus, red
Hair on the back of the hands, unreal
Heraldic axe in the hands.

Unreal but still can strike.
And in defence we cannot call on the evening
Or the seeming-friendly woods —
Nature is not to be trusted,

Nature whose falls of snow,
Falling softer than catkins,
Bury the lost and over their grave a distant
Smile spreads in the sun.

Not to be trusted, no,
Deaf at the best; she is only
And always herself, Nature is only herself,
Only the shadows longer and longer.

Night Club

After the legshows and the brandies
And all the pick-me-ups for tired
Men there is a feeling
Something more is required.

The lights go down and eyes
Look up across the room;
Salome comes in, bearing
The head of God knows whom.

The Dowser

An inkling only, whisper in the bones
Of strange weather on the way,
Twitch of the eyelid, shadow of a passing bird.
It is coming some time soon.

What? or who? An inkling only,
Adumbration of unknown glory
Drew to the feet of Saint Francis where the waves
Broke, an army of fish.

Humming wires; feel of a lost limb
Cut off in another life;
Trance on the tripod; effulgence
Of headlights beyond the rise in the road.

And the hazel rod bent, dipping, contorting,
Snake from sleep; they were right
Who remembered some old fellow
(Dead long ago) who remembered the well.

'Dig', he said, 'dig',
Holding the lantern, the rod bent double,
And we dug respecting his knowledge,
Not waiting for morning, keenly

Dug: the clay was heavy
Two hours heavy before
The clink of a spade revealed
What or whom? We expected a well —

A well? A mistake somewhere . . .
More of a tomb . . . Anyway we backed away
From the geyser suddenly of light that erupted, sprayed
Rocketing over the sky azaleas and gladioli.

Prayer before Birth

I am not yet born; O hear me.
Let not the bloodsucking bat or the rat or the stoat or the
 club-footed ghoul come near me.

I am not yet born, console me.
I fear that the human race may with tall walls wall me,
 with strong drugs dope me, with wise lies lure me,
 on black racks rack me, in blood-baths roll me.

I am not yet born; provide me
With water to dandle me, grass to grow for me, trees to talk
 to me, sky to sing to me, birds and a white light
 in the back of my mind to guide me.

I am not yet born; forgive me
For the sins that in me the world shall commit, my words
 when they speak me, my thoughts when they think me,
 my treason engendered by traitors beyond me,
 my life when they murder by means of my
 hands, my death when they live me.

I am not yet born; rehearse me
In the parts I must play and the cues I must take when
 old men lecture me, bureaucrats hector me, mountains
 frown at me, lovers laugh at me, the white
 waves call me to folly and the desert calls
 me to doom and the beggar refuses
 my gift and my children curse me.

I am not yet born; O hear me,
Let not the man who is beast or who thinks he is God
 come near me.

I am not yet born; O fill me
With strength against those who would freeze my
    humanity, would dragoon me into a lethal automaton,
        would make me a cog in a machine, a thing with
            one face, a thing, and against all those
                who would dissipate my entirety, would
                    blow me like thistledown hither and
                        thither or hither and thither
                            like water held in the
                                hands would spill me.

Let them not make me a stone and let them not spill me.
Otherwise kill me.

Troll's Courtship

I am a lonely Troll after my gala night;
I have knocked down houses and stamped my feet on the people's
    heart,
I have trundled round the sky with the executioner's cart
And dropped my bait for corpses, watched them bite,
But I am a lonely Troll — nothing in the end comes right.

In a smoking and tinkling dawn with fires and broken glass
I am a lonely Troll; my tributes are in vain
To Her to whom if I had even a human brain
I might have reached but, as it is, the epochs pass
And leave me unfulfilled, no further than I was.

Because I cannot accurately conceive
Any ideal, even ideal Death,
My curses and my boasts are merely a waste of breath,
My lusts and lonelinesses grunt and heave
And blunder round among the ruins that I leave.

Yet from the lubber depths of my unbeing I
Aspire to Her who was my Final Cause but who
Is always somewhere else and not to be spoken to,
Is always nowhere: which is in the long run why
I make for nowhere, make a shambles of the sky.

Nostalgia for the breasts that never gave nor could
Give milk or even warmth has desolated me,
Clutching at shadows of my nullity
That slink and mutter through the leafless wood
Which thanks to me is dead, is dead for good.

A cone of ice enclosing liquid fire,
Utter negation in a positive form,
That would be how She is, the nadir and the norm
Of dissolution and the constant pyre
Of all desirable things — that is what I desire

And therefore cry to Her with the voice of broken bells
To come, visibly, palpably, to come,
Gluing my ear to gutted walls but walls are dumb,
All I can catch is a gurgle as of the sea in shells
But not Her voice — for She is always somewhere else.

Neutrality

The neutral island facing the Atlantic,
The neutral island in the heart of man,
Are bitterly soft reminders of the beginnings
That ended before the end began.

Look into your heart, you will find a County Sligo,
A Knocknarea with for navel a cairn of stones,
You will find the shadow and sheen of a moleskin mountain
And a litter of chronicles and bones.

Look into your heart, you will find fermenting rivers,
Intricacies of gloom and glint,
You will find such ducats of dream and great doubloons of
    ceremony
As nobody today would mint.

But then look eastward from your heart, there bulks
A continent, close, dark, as archetypal sin,
While to the west off your own shores the mackerel
Are fat — on the flesh of your kin.

The Mixer

With a pert moustache and a ready candid smile
He has played his way through twenty years of pubs,
Deckchairs, lounges, touchlines, junctions, homes,
And still as ever popular, he roams
Far and narrow, mimicking the style
Of other people's leisure, scattering stubs.

Colourless, when alone, and self-accused,
He is only happy in reflected light
And only real in the range of laughter;
Behind his eyes are shadows of a night
In Flanders but his mind long since refused
To let that time intrude on what came after.

So in this second war which is fearful too,
He cannot away with silence but has grown
Almost a cypher, like a Latin word
That many languages have made their own
Till it is worn and blunt and easy to construe
And often spoken but no longer heard.

Nostalgia

In cock-wattle sunset or grey
Dawn when the dagger
Points again of longing
For what was never home
We needs must turn away
From the voices that cry 'Come' —
That under-sea ding-donging.

Dingle-dongle, bells and bluebells,
Snapdragon solstice, lunar lull,
The wasp circling the honey
Or the lamp soft on the snow —
These are the times at which
The will is vulnerable,
The trigger-finger slow,
The spirit lonely.

These are the times at which
Aloneness is too ripe
When homesick for the hollow
Heart of the Milky Way
The soundless clapper calls
And we would follow
But earth and will are stronger
And nearer — and we stay.

When we were Children

When we were children words were coloured
(Harlot and murder were dark purple)
And language was a prism, the light
    A conjured inlay on the grass,
Whose rays today are concentrated
    And language grown a burning-glass.

When we were children Spring was easy,
Dousing our heads in suds of hawthorn
And scrambling the laburnum tree —
    A breakfast for the gluttonous eye;
Whose winds and sweets have now forsaken
    Lungs that are black, tongues that are dry.

Now we are older and our talents
Accredited to time and meaning,
To handsel joy requires a new
    Shuffle of cards behind the brain
Where meaning shall remarry colour
    And flowers be timeless once again.

Corner Seat

Suspended in a moving night
The face in the reflected train
Looks at first sight as self-assured
As your own face — But look again:
Windows between you and the world
Keep out the cold, keep out the fright;
Then why does your reflection seem
So lonely in the moving night?

Littoral

Indigo, mottle of purple and amber, ink,
Damson whipped with cream, improbable colours of sea
And unanalysable rhythms — fingering foam
Tracing, erasing its runes, regardless
Of you and me
And whether we think it escape or the straight way home.

The sand here looks like metal, it feels there like fur,
The wind films the sand with sand;
This hoary beach is burgeoning with minutiae
Like a philosopher
Who, thinking, makes cat's-cradles with string — or a widow
Who knits for her sons but remembers a tomb in another land.

Brain-bound or heart-bound sea — old woman or old man —
To whom we are ciphers, creatures to ignore,
We poach from you what images we can,
Luxuriously afraid
To plump the Unknown in a bucket with a spade —
Each child his own seashore.

The Cromlech

From trivia of froth and pollen
White tufts in the rabbit warren
And every minute like a ticket
Nicked and dropped, nicked and dropped,
Extracters and abstracters ask
What emerges, what survives,
And once the stopper is unstopped
What was the essence in the flask
And what is Life apart from lives
And where, apart from fact, the value

To which we answer, being naïve,
Wearing the world upon our sleeve,
That to dissect a given thing
Unravelling its complexity
Outrages its simplicity
For essence is not merely core
And each event implies the world,
A centre needs periphery.

This being so, at times at least
Granted the sympathetic pulse
And granted the perceiving eye
Each pregnant with a history,
Appearance and appearances —
In spite of the philosophers
With their jejune dichotomies —
Can be at times reality.

So Tom and Tessy holding hands
(Dare an abstraction steal a kiss?)
Cannot be generalized away,
Reduced by bleak analysis
To pointers demonstrating laws
Which drain the colour from the day;
Not mere effects of a crude cause

But of themselves significant,
To rule-of-brain recalcitrant,
This that they are and do is This . . .

Tom is here, Tessy is here
At this point in a given year
With all this hour's accessories,
A given glory — and to look
That gift-horse in the mouth will prove
Or disprove nothing of their love
Which is as sure intact a fact,
Though young and supple, as what stands
Obtuse and old, in time congealed,
Behind them as they mingle hands —
Self-contained, unexplained,
The cromlech in the clover field.

Under the Mountain

Seen from above
The foam in the curving bay is a goose-quill
That feathers . . . unfeathers . . . itself.

Seen from above
The field is a flap and the haycocks buttons
To keep it flush with the earth.

Seen from above
The house is a silent gadget whose purpose
Was long since obsolete.

But when you get down
The breakers are cold scum and the wrack
Sizzles with stinking life.

When you get down
The field is a failed or a worth-while crop, the source
Of back-ache if not heartache.

And when you get down
The house is a maelstrom of loves and hates where you —
Having got down — belong.

Aubade for Infants

Snap the blind; I am not blind,
I must spy what stalks behind
Wall and window — Something large
Is barging up beyond the down,
Chirruping, hooting, hot of foot.

Beyond that wall what things befall?
My eye can fly though I must crawl.
Dance and dazzle — Something bright
Ignites the dumps of sodden cloud,
Loud and laughing, a fiery face . . .

Whose broad grimace (the voice is bass)
Makes nonsense of my time and place —
Maybe you think that I am young?
I who flung before my birth
To mother earth the dawn-song too!

And you —
However old and deaf this year —
Were near me when that song was sung.

The Cyclist

Freewheeling down the escarpment past the unpassing horse
Blazoned in chalk the wind he causes in passing
Cools the sweat of his neck, making him one with the sky,
In the heat of the handlebars he grasps the summer
Being a boy and to-day a parenthesis
Between the horizon's brackets; the main sentence
Is to be picked up later but these five minutes
Are all to-day and summer. The dragonfly
Rises without take-off, horizontal,
Underlining itself in a sliver of peacock light.

And glaring, glaring white
The horse on the down moves within his brackets,
The grass boils with grasshoppers, a pebble
Scutters from under the wheel and all this country
Is spattered white with boys riding their heat-wave,
Feet on a narrow plank and hair thrown back

And a surf of dust beneath them. Summer, summer —
They chase it with butterfly nets or strike it into the deep
In a little red ball or gulp it lathered with cream
Or drink it through closed eyelids; until the bell
Left-right-left gives his forgotten sentence
And reaching the valley the boy must pedal again
Left-right-left but meanwhile
For ten seconds more can move as the horse in the chalk
Moves unbeginningly calmly
Calmly regardless of tenses and final clauses
Calmly unendingly moves.

Woods

My father who found the English landscape tame
Had hardly in his life walked in a wood,
Too old when first he met one; Malory's knights,
Keats's nymphs or the Midsummer Night's Dream
Could never arras the room, where he spelled out True and Good
With their interleaving of half-truths and not-quites.

While for me from the age of ten the socketed wooden gate
Into a Dorset planting, into a dark
But gentle ambush, was an alluring eye;
Within was a kingdom free from time and sky,
Caterpillar webs on the forehead, danger under the feet,
And the mind adrift in a floating and rustling ark

Packed with birds and ghosts, two of every race,
Trills of love from the picture-book — Oh might I never land
But here, grown six foot tall, find me also a love
Also out of the picture-book; whose hand
Would be soft as the webs of the wood and on her face
The wood-pigeon's voice would shaft a chrism from above.

So in a grassy ride a rain-filled hoof-mark coined
By a finger of sun from the mint of Long Ago
Was the last of Lancelot's glitter. Make-believe dies hard;
That the rider passed here lately and is a man we know
Is still untrue, the gate to Legend remains unbarred,
The grown-up hates to divorce what the child joined.

Thus from a city when my father would frame
Escape, he thought, as I do, of bog or rock
But I have also this other, this English, choice
Into what yet is foreign; whatever its name
Each wood is the mystery and the recurring shock
Of its dark coolness is a foreign voice.

Yet in using the word tame my father was maybe right,
These woods are not the Forest; each is moored
To a village somewhere near. If not of to-day
They are not like the wilds of Mayo, they are assured
Of their place by men; reprieved from the neolithic night
By gamekeepers or by Herrick's girls at play.

And always we walk out again. The patch
Of sky at the end of the path grows and discloses
An ordered open air long ruled by dyke and fence,
With geese whose form and gait proclaim their consequence,
Pargetted outposts, windows browed with thatch,
And cow pats — and inconsequent wild roses.

Autolycus

In his last phase when hardly bothering
To be a dramatist, the Master turned away
From his taut plots and complex characters
To tapestried romances, conjuring
With rainbow names and handfuls of sea-spray
And from them turned out happy Ever-afters.

Eclectic always, now extravagant,
Sighting his matter through a timeless prism
He ranged his classical bric-à-brac in grottos
Where knights of Ancient Greece had Latin mottoes
And fishermen their flapjacks — none should want
Colour for lack of an anachronism.

A gay world certainly though pocked and scored
With childish horrors and a fresh world though
Its mainsprings were old gags — babies exposed,
Identities confused and queens to be restored;
But when the cracker bursts it proves as you supposed —
Trinket and moral tumble out just so.

Such innocence — In his own words it was
Like an old tale, only that where time leaps
Between acts three and four there was something born
Which made the stock-type virgin dance like corn
In a wind that having known foul marshes, barren steeps,
Felt therefore kindly towards Marinas, Perditas . . .

Thus crystal learned to talk. But Shakespeare balanced it
With what we knew already, gabbing earth
Hot from Eastcheap — Watch your pockets when
That rogue comes round the corner, he can slit
Purse-strings as quickly as his maker's pen
Will try your heartstrings in the name of mirth.

O master pedlar with your confidence tricks,
Brooches, pomanders, broadsheets and what-have-you,
Who hawk such entertainment but rook your client
And leave him brooding, why should we forgive you
Did we not know that, though more self-reliant
Than we, you too were born and grew up in a fix?

Hands and Eyes

In a high wind
Gnarled hands cup to kindle an old briar,
From a frilled cot
Twin sea anemones grope for a hanging lamp,
In a foul cage
Old coal-gloves dangle from dejected arms.

Of which three pairs of hands the child's are helpless
(Whose wheels barely engage)
And the shepherd's from his age are almost bloodless
While the chimpanzee's are hopeless
Were there not even a cage.

In a dark room
Docile pupils grow to their full for prey,
Down a long bar
Mascara scrawls a gloss on a torn leaf,
On a high col
The climber's blue marries the blue he climbs.

Of which three pairs of eyes the tart's are mindless
(Who pawned her mind elsewhere)
And the black cat's, in gear with black, are heartless
While the alpinist's are timeless
In gear with timeless air.

In a cold church
It flickers in the draught, then burns erect;
In a loud mob
It bulges, merges, feels with a start alone;
In a bright beam
It waltzes dust to dust with its chance loves.

Of which three souls the praying one is selfless
But only for a span
And the gregarious man's is rudderless, powerless,
While the soul in love is luckless,
Betrays what chance it can.

And still the wind
Blows, the ape is marooned, the lamp ungrasped;
Woman and cat
Still wait to pounce and the climber waits to fall;
As each soul burns
The best it may, in foul or blustering air.
Oh would He, were there a God, have mercy on us all?

Slow Movement

Waking, he found himself in a train, andante,
With wafers of early sunlight blessing the unknown fields
And yesterday cancelled out, except for yesterday's papers
    Huddling under the seat.

It is still very early, this is a slow movement;
The viola-player's hand like a fish in a glass tank
Rises, remains quivering, darts away
    To nibble invisible weeds.

Great white nebulae lurch against the window
To deploy across the valley, the children are not yet up
To wave us on — we pass without spectators,
    Braiding a voiceless creed.

And the girl opposite, name unknown, is still
Asleep and the colour of her eyes unknown
Which might be wells of sun or moons of wish
    But it is still very early.

The movement ends, the train has come to a stop
In buttercup fields, the fiddles are silent, the whole
Shoal of silver tessellates the aquarium
    Floor, not a bubble rises . . .

And what happens next on the programme we do not know,
If, the red line topped on the gauge, the fish will go mad in the tank
Accelerando con forza, the sleeper open her eyes
    And, so doing, open ours.

Western Landscape

In doggerel and stout let me honour this country
Though the air is so soft that it smudges the words
And herds of great clouds find the gaps in the fences
Of chance preconceptions and foam-quoits on rock-points
At once hit and miss, hit and miss.
So the kiss of the past is narcotic, the ocean
Lollingly lullingly over-insidiously
Over and under crossing the eyes
And docking the queues of the teetotum consciousness
Proves and disproves what it wants.
For the western climate is Lethe,
The smoky taste of cooking on turf is lotus,
There are affirmation and abnegation together
From the broken bog with its veins of amber water,
From the distant headland, a sphinx's fist, that barely grips the sea,
From the taut-necked donkey's neurotic-asthmatic-erotic
     lamenting,
From the heron in trance and in half-mourning,
From the mitred mountain weeping shale.
O grail of emerald passing light
And hanging smell of sweetest hay
And grain of sea and loom of wind
Weavingly laughingly leavingly weepingly —
Webs that will last and will not.
But what
Is the hold upon, the affinity with
Ourselves of such a light and line,
How do we find continuance
Of our too human skeins of wish
In this inhuman effluence?
O relevance of cloud and rock —
If such could be our permanence!
The flock of mountain sheep belong
To tumbled screes, to tumbling seas
The ribboned wrack, and moor to mist;
But we who savour longingly

This plenitude of solitude
Have lost the right to residence,
Can only glean ephemeral
Ears of our once beatitude.
Caressingly cajolingly —
Take what you can for soon you go —
Consolingly, coquettishly,
The soft rain kisses and forgets,
Silken mesh on skin and mind;
A deaf-dumb siren that can sing
With fingertips her falsities,
Welcoming, abandoning.

O Brandan, spindrift hermit, who
Hankering roaming un-homing up-anchoring
From this rock wall looked seawards to
Knot the horizon round your waist,
Distil that distance and undo
Time in a quintessential West:
The best negation, round as nought,
Stiller than stolen sleep — though bought
With mortification, voiceless choir
Where all were silent as one man
And all desire fulfilled, unsought.
Thought:
The curragh went over the wave and dipped in the trough
When that horny-handed saint with the abstract eye set off
Which was fourteen hundred years ago — maybe never —
And yet he bobs beyond the next high crest for ever.
Feeling:
Sea met sky, he had neither floor nor ceiling,
The rising blue of turf-smoke and mountain were left behind,
Blue neither upped nor downed, there was blue all round the mind.
Emotion:
One thought of God, one feeling of the ocean,
Fused in the moving body, the unmoved soul,
Made him a part of a nut to be parted whole.
Whole.

And the West was all the world, the lonely was the only,
The chosen — and there was no choice — the Best,
For the beyond was here . . .

                                        But for us now
The beyond is still out there as on tiptoes here we stand
On promontories that are themselves a-tiptoe
Reluctant to be land. Which is why this land
Is always more than matter — as a ballet
Dancer is more than body. The west of Ireland
Is brute and ghost at once. Therefore in passing
Among these shadows of this permanent show
Flitting evolving dissolving but never quitting —
This arbitrary and necessary Nature
Both bountiful and callous, harsh and wheedling —
Let now the visitor, although disfranchised
In the constituencies of quartz and bog-oak
And ousted from the elemental congress,
Let me at least in token that my mother
Earth was a rocky earth with breasts uncovered
To suckle solitary intellects
And limber instincts, let me, if a bastard
Out of the West by urban civilization
(Which unwished father claims me — so I must take
What I can before I go) let me who am neither Brandan
Free of all roots nor yet a rooted peasant
Here add one stone to the indifferent cairn . . .
With a stone on the cairn, with a word on the wind, with a prayer
    in the flesh let me honour this country.

Mahabalipuram

All alone from his dark sanctum the lingam fronts, affronts the sea,
The world's dead weight of breakers against sapling, bull and
    candle
        Where worship comes no more,
Yet how should these cowherds and gods continue to dance in the
    rock
All the long night along ocean in this lost border between
That thronging gonging mirage of paddy and toddy and dung
        And this uninhabited shore?

Silent except for the squadrons of water, the dark grim chargers
    launched from Australia,
Dark except for their manes of phosphorus, silent in spite of the
    rockhewn windmill
        That brandishes axe and knife —
The many-handed virgin facing, abasing the Oaf, the Demon;
Dark in spite of the rockhewn radiance of Vishnu and Shiva and
    silent
In spite of the mooing of Krishna's herds; yet in spite of this
    darkness and silence
        Behold what a joy of life —

Which goes with an awe and a horror; the innocence which
    surmounted the guilt
Thirteen centuries back when an artist eyeing this litter of granite
        Saw it for waste and took
A header below the rockface, found there already like a ballet of
    fishes
Passing, repassing each other, these shapes of gopi and goblin,
Of elephant, serpent and antelope, saw them and grasped his
    mallet
        And cried with a clear stroke: Look!

And now we look, we to whom mantra and mudra mean little,
And who find in this Hindu world a zone that is ultra-violet
      Balanced by an infra-red,
Austerity and orgy alike being phrased, it seems, in a strange dead
    language
But now that we look without trying to learn and only look in the
    act of leaping
After the sculptor into the rockface, now we can see, if not hear,
    those phrases
      To be neither strange nor dead.

Not strange for all their farouche iconography, not so strange as our
    own dreams
Because better ordered, these are the dreams we have needed
      Since we forgot how to dance;
This god asleep on the snake is the archetype of the sleep that we
    lost
When we were born, and these wingless figures that fly
Merely by bending the knee are the earnest of what we aspire to
      Apart from science and chance.

And the largest of all these reliefs, forty foot high by a hundred,
Is large in more senses than one, including both heaven and the
    animal kingdom
      And a grain of salt as well
For the saint stands always above on one leg fasting
Acquiring power while the smug hypocritical cat beneath him
Stands on his hindlegs too admired by the mice
      Whom the sculptor did not tell.

Nor did he tell the simple and beautiful rustics
Who saved from their doom by Krishna are once more busy and
    happy
      Absorbed in themselves and Him,
That trapped in this way in the rock their idyl would live to excite
And at once annul the lust and the envy of tourists
Taking them out of themselves and to find themselves in a world
      That has neither rift nor rim:

A monochrome world that has all the indulgence of colour,
A still world whose every harmonic is audible,
          Largesse of spirit and stone;
Created things for once and for all featured in full while for once
      and never
The creator who is destroyer stands at the last point of land
Featureless; in a dark cell, a phallus of granite, as abstract
          As the North Pole; as alone.

But the visitor must move on and the waves assault the temple,
Living granite against dead water, and time with its weathering
      action
          Make phrase and feature blurred;
Still from today we know what an avatar is, we have seen
God take shape and dwell among shapes, we have felt
Our ageing limbs respond to those ageless limbs in the rock
          Reliefs. Relief is the word.

The Window

I

Neck of an hour-glass on its side —
  Hermitage, equilibrium.
The slightest tilt and a grain would glide
  Away from you or towards you;
So without tremolo hold this moment
  Where in this window two worlds meet
Or family voices from the room behind you
Or canned music from beyond the garden
  Will irrupt, disrupt, delete.

Between this room and the open air
  Flowers in a vase imponderably —
The painter knew who set them there
  The knack of closed and open;
With highlights upon bloom and bulge
  He hung this bridge in timelessness
Preventing traffic hence and hither
And claimed his own authority
  To span, to ban, to bless.

The sands of light within, without,
  Equated and inviolable,
Allow no footprint and no doubt
  Of savagery or trespass
Where art enhancing yet revoking
  The random lives on which it drew
Has centred round a daub of ochre,
Has garnered in a square of canvas
  Something complete and new.

So there it rests the clump of flowers,
  Suspension bridge and talisman,
Not his nor hers nor yours nor ours
  But everyone's and no one's,

Against the light, flanked by the curtains
  No draught nor chatter can discompose
For this is a window we cannot open
A hair's breadth more, this is a window
  Impossible to close.

Thus pictures (windows themselves) preclude
  Both ventilation and burglary —
No entrance to their solitude,
  No egress to adventure,
For life that lives from mind to moment,
  From mouth to mouth, from none to now,
Must never, they say, infringe that circle,
At most may sense it at a tangent
  And without knowing how.

II

How, yes how! To achieve in a world of flux and bonfires
Something of art's coherence, in a world of wind and hinges
An even approximate poise, in a world of beds and hunger
  A fullness more than the feeding a sieve?
For the windows here admit draughts and the bridges may not be
    loitered on
And what was ecstasy there would be quietism here and the people
  Here have to live.

Beginning your life with an overdraft, born looking out on a surge
    of eroding
Objects, your cradle a coracle, your eyes when they start to focus
Traitors to the king within you, born in the shadow of an hour-
    glass
  But vertical (this is not art),
We feel like the tides the tug of a moon, never to be reached,
    interfering always,
And always we suffer this two-way traffic, impulses outward and
    images inward
  Distracting the heart.

And the infant's eyes are drawn to the blank of light, the window,
The small boy cranes out to spit on the pavement, the student tosses
His midnight thoughts to the wind, the schoolgirl ogles the
    brilliantined
  Head that dazzles the day
While the bedridden general stares and stares, embarking
On a troopship of cloud for his youth or for Landikotal, evading
  The sneer of the medicine tray.

Take-off outwards and over and through the same channel an
    intake —
Thistledown, dust in the sun, fritillaries, homing pigeons,
All to which senses and mind like sea anemones open
  In this never private pool;
The waves of other men's bodies and minds galumphing in,
    voices demanding
To be heard or be silenced, complied with, competed with,
    answered,
  Voices that flummox and fool,

That nonchalantly beguile or bark like a sergeant-major,
Narcotic voices like bees in a buddleia bush or neurotic
Screaming of brakes and headlines, voices that grab through the
    window
  And chivvy us out and on
To make careers, make love, to dunk our limbs in tropical
Seas, or to buy and sell in the temple from which the angry
  Man with the whip has gone.

He has gone and the others go too but still there is often a face at
    your window —
The Welsh corporal who sang in the pub, the girl who was always
    at a cross purpose,
The pilot doodling at his last briefing, the Catalan women
    clutching the soup bowl,
  The child that has not been born:
All looking in and their eyes meet yours, the hour-glass turns over
    and lies level,

The stopwatch clicks, the sand stops trickling, what was remote
    and raw is blended
    And mended what was torn.

And how between inrush and backwash such a betrothal should
    happen
Of tethered antennae and drifting vanishing filament
We do not know nor who keeps the ring and in passing
    Absolves us from time and tide
And from our passing selves, who salves from the froth of otherness
These felt and delectable Others; we do not know for we lose
    ourselves
    In finding a world outside.

Loss and discovery, froth and fulfilment, this is our medium,
A second best, an approximate, frameless, a sortie, a tentative
Counter attack on the void, a launching forth from the window
    Of a raven or maybe a dove
And we do not know what they will find but gambling on their
    fidelity
And on other islanded lives we keep open the window and fallibly
    Await the return of love.

III

How, yes how? In this mirrored maze —
    Paradox and antinomy —
To card the bloom off falling days,
    To reach the core that answers?
And how on the edge of senselessness
    To team and build, to mate and breed,
Forcing the mud to dance a ballet,
Consigning an old and doubtful cargo
    To a new and wayward seed?

But, hows apart, this we affirm
    (Pentecost or sacrament?)
That though no frame will hold, no term
    Describe our Pyrrhic salvoes,

Yet that which art gleaning, congealing,
  Sets in antithesis to life
Is what in living we lay claim to,
Is what gives light and shade to living
  Though not with brush or knife.

The painted curtain never stirs —
  Airlessness and hourlessness —
And a dead painter still demurs
  When we intrude our selfhood;
But even as he can talk by silence
  So, blinkered and acquisitive,
Even at the heart of lust and conflict
We can find form, our lives transcended
  While and because we live.

But here our jargon fails; no word,
  'Miracle' or 'catalysis',
Will fit what dare not have occurred
  But does occur regardless;
Let then the poet like the parent
  Take it on trust and, looking out
Through his own window to where others
Look out at him, be proudly humbled
  And jettison his doubt.

The air blows in, the pigeons cross —
  Communication! Alchemy!
Here is profit where was loss
  And what were dross are golden,
Those are friends who now were foreign
  And gentler shines the face of doom,
The pot of flowers inspires the window,
The air blows in, the vistas open
  And a sweet scent pervades the room.

from *Donegal Triptych*

I

Broken bollard, rusted hawser,
Age-old reasons for new rhyme,
Bring forward now their backward time:
The glad sad poetry of departure.

But arrival? Go your furthest,
The Muse unpacks herself in prose;
Once arrived, the clocks disclose
That each arrival means returning.

Returning where? To speak of cycles
Rings as false as moving straight
Since the gimlet of our fate
Makes all life, all love, a spiral.

Here for instance: lanes of fuchsias
Bleed such hills as, earlier mine,
Vanished later; later shine
More than ever, with my collusion.

And more and mine than ever, the rumpled
Tigers of the bogland streams
Prowl and plunge through glooms and gleams
To merge their separate whims in wonder;

While the sea still counts her sevens
And the wind still spreads his white
Muslin over the strand, and night
Closes down as dense as ever.

But who has turned the screw? We are further
Off. Or is it deeper in?
All our ends once more begin,
All our depth usurps our surface.

Surface takes a glossier polish,
Depth a richer gloom. And steel
Skewers the heart. Our fingers feel
The height of the sky, the ocean bottom.

Yet the cold voice chops and sniggers,
Prosing on, maintains the thread
Is broken and the phoenix fled,
Youth and poetry departed.

The Once-in-Passing

And here the cross on the window means myself
But that window does not open;
Born here, I should have proved a different self.
Such vistas dare not open;
For what can walk or talk without tongue or feet?

Here for a month to spend but not to earn,
How could I even imagine
Such a life here that my plain days could earn
The life my dreams imagine?
For what takes root or grows that owns no root?

Yet here for a month, and for this once in passing,
I can imagine at least
The permanence of what passes,
As though the window opened
And the ancient cross on the hillside meant myself.

The Here-and-Never

Here it was here and now, but never
There and now or here and then.
Ragweed grows where a house dies
Whose children are no longer children
And what you see when you close your eyes
Is here and never: never again.

Here it was coming and going, but never
Coming the same, or the same gone.
New York is not so far by post,
Yet the posted photograph seems only
The twitch of a corpse, the gift of a ghost,
The winter of a spring that shone.

Here it was living and dying, but never
Lifelong dying or dead-alive.
Few were few but all knew all,
The all were few and therefore many,
Landscape and seascape at one's call,
The senses five or more than five.

So now, which here should mean for ever,
And here which now is the Now of men,
They come and go, they live and die,
Ruins to rock but rock to houses,
And here means now to the opened eye
And both mean ever, though never again.

Wessex Guidebook

Hayfoot; strawfoot; the illiterate seasons
Still clump their way through Somerset and Dorset
While George the Third still rides his horse of chalk
From Weymouth and the new salt water cure
Towards Windsor and incurable madness. Inland
The ghosts of monks have grown too fat to walk
Through bone-dry ruins plugged with fossil sea-shells.

Thou shalt! Thou shalt not! In the yellow abbey
Inscribed beneath the crossing the Ten Commandments
Are tinted red by a Fifteenth Century fire;
On one round hill the yews still furnish bows
For Agincourt while, equally persistent,
Beneath another, in green-grassed repose,
Arthur still waits the call to rescue Britain.

Flake-tool; core-tool; in the small museum
Rare butterflies, green coins of Caracalla,
Keep easy company with the fading hand
Of one who chronicled a fading world;
Outside, the long roads, that the Roman ruler
Ruled himself out with, point across the land
To lasting barrows and long vanished barracks.

And thatchpoll numskull rows of limestone houses,
Dead from the navel down in plate glass windows,
Despise their homebrewed past, ignore the clock
On the village church in deference to Big Ben
Who booms round china dog and oaken settle
Announcing it is time and time again
To plough up tumuli, to damn the hindmost.

But hindmost, topmost, those illiterate seasons
Still smoke their pipes in swallow-hole and hide-out
As scornful of the tractor and the jet
As of the Roman road, or axe of flint,

Forgotten by the mass of human beings
Whom they, the Seasons, need not even forget
Since, though they fostered man, they never loved him.

Beni Hasan

It came to me on the Nile my passport lied
Calling me dark who am grey. In the brown cliff
A row of tombs, of portholes, stared and stared as if
They were the long dead eyes of beasts inside
Time's cage, black eyes on eyes that stared away
Lion-like focused on some different day
On which, on a long term view, it was I, not they, had died.

from *Jigsaws*

IV

Fresh from the knife and coming to,
I asked myself could this be I
They had just cut up. 'Oh no, not you,
Certainly not!' came the reply;
'The operation must have veered
Off course, had not some nameless stranger
Entering your body volunteered,
Hand in glove, to share your danger.'

But hand in glove! one cell from two!
I thought, when stronger, I must ask
Who is this, ramifying through
My veins, who wears me like a mask —
Or is it I wear him? One week
Later I found that I could spare
The strength to ask, but did not speak.
That stranger was no longer there.

V

Although we say we disbelieve,
God comes in handy when we swear —
It may be when we exult or grieve,
It may be just to clear the air;
Let the skew runner breast the tape,
Let the great lion leave his lair,
Let the hot nymph solicit rape,
We need a God to phrase it fair;
When death curls over in the wave
Strings may soar and brass may blare
But, to be frightened or be brave,
We crave some emblem for despair,
And when ice burns and joys are pain
And shadows grasp us by the hair
We need one Name to take in vain,
One taboo to break, one sin to dare.
What is it then we disbelieve?
Because the facts are far from bare
And all religions must deceive
And every proof must wear and tear,
That God exists we cannot show,
So do not know but need not care.
Thank God we do not know; we know
We need the unknown. The Unknown is There.

The Other Wing

Rat-tat-tat-tash of shields upon Ida
Among pellmell rocks and harum-scarum
Ibex and tettix; willy-nilly
The infant cried while the tenterhook heaven
Cranes through the cracks of its blue enamel
To spot the usurper but metal on metal
Drowns him and saves him, drowns and saves.

Who later, enthroned in his talk-happy heaven,
Felt suddenly harassed, a sky-splitting headache
With nothing to cause it — and out of that nothing
Hard-eyed and helmeted vaulted a goddess;
A shuttle flew like a clacking fish,
A long spear flew, and the journeymen artists
Weighed her in stone, wooed her in stone.

Or in bronze or chryselephant; hence these muted
Miles of parquet, these careful lights,
This aquarium of conditioned air,
This ne plus ultra. Ultra? But yes,
Gentlemen, first on the left beyond these
Black figure vases there lies a red
Letter or birth day, another wing. . . .

Where are two grubs: one like a sentry
In a tall box, at attention, lagged in his
Mummicose death-dress; one much smaller
Lagged against life — he too has a Mary
But never a Martha to tidy the stables,
Poor Tom o' Bethlehem, only a Mary,
An ox and an ass, a nought and a cross

Whose ways will cross, over and over,
The centuries unwinding the swaddling
Bands and the death-bands; the long thin pupa
Always must wait for the small round one,
Deaf till the warm voice cure him, but Tom
Condemned to another, a haunted, wing,
For all his fire poor Tom's a-cold.

The Burnt Bridge

So, passing through the rustic gate,
He slammed it to (it broke in two)
As he took quick strides to tempt his fate
And the world ahead was daylight.

But when he reached the haunted coombe,
Glancing left, glancing right,
On either ridge he glimpsed his doom
And the world ahead was darkness.

He slept aloft on a sarsen stone
Dreaming to, dreaming fro,
And the more he dreamt was the more alone
And the future seemed behind him.

But waking stiff and scrambling down
At the first light, the cramped light,
The wood below him seemed to frown
And the past deployed before him;

For his long-lost dragon lurked ahead,
Not to be dodged and never napping,
And he knew in his bones he was all but dead,
Yet that death was half the story.

Still he clambered through the barbed wire fence
Into the wood and against his will
And the air in the wood was dark and tense,
The world was tense and tortured.

So on he went and the wood went on,
With boughs a-creak, with birds a-croak,
But where, thought he, had his dragon gone?
Where had he gone and wherefore?

Yet he picked his steps and the wood passed by,
The world drew breath, the sun was safe,
When a shining river caught his eye
With a bridge and a shining lady.

She stood where the water bubbled bright
On the near bank, the known bank;
He took her hand and they struck a light
And crossed that bridge and burnt it.

And went to the west, went hand in hand,
(And hand in hand went song and silence)
Till they thought they saw the golden strand
Of the sea that leads to nowhere.

But was it strand? Or was it sea?
As near they came it went as far.
Dragons? she said, Let dragons be;
Those waves ahead are shoreless.

So, far they came and found no shore,
The waves falling, the night falling,
To board a ship sunk years before
And all the world was daylight.

House on a Cliff

Indoors the tang of a tiny oil lamp. Outdoors
The winking signal on the waste of sea.
Indoors the sound of the wind. Outdoors the wind.
Indoors the locked heart and the lost key.

Outdoors the chill, the void, the siren. Indoors
The strong man pained to find his red blood cools,
While the blind clock grows louder, faster. Outdoors
The silent moon, the garrulous tides she rules.

Indoors ancestral curse-cum-blessing. Outdoors
The empty bowl of heaven, the empty deep.
Indoors a purposeful man who talks at cross
Purposes, to himself, in a broken sleep.

Figure of Eight

In the top and front of a bus, eager to meet his fate,
He pressed with foot and mind to gather speed,
Then, when the lights were changing, jumped and hurried,
Though dead on time, to the meeting place agreed,
But there was no one there. He chose to wait.
No one came. He need not perhaps have worried.

Whereas to-day in the rear and gloom of a train,
Loath, loath to meet his fate, he cowers and prays
For some last-minute hitch, some unheard-of abdication,
But, winding up the black thread of his days,
The wheels roll on and make it all too plain
Who will be there to meet him at the station.

from *Visitations*

I

Never so lithe in the green dingle,
Never so ripe in the grown hay,
The ghosts of pastoral tease and mingle
With darker ghosts from that dark day
Which means our own. Your own? say they;
How can you prove your minds are single
Or, muted words from worlds away
Setting both ears and nerves a-tingle,
Tell what your ears and nerves obey?

Never so young in their green fettle,
Never so glad in their gleaned light,
Never so proud in pulse and petal,
So much themselves in despite of spite,
Look, they come back; and, burning bright,
Turn roof and tree to dazzling metal
Transmuting all our greys to white
And, when our night begins to settle,
Divulge their day to shame our night.

Never so innocent of lying,
Never so gay in blood and bone,
Never with more that is worth the buying,
Never with less for which to atone,
Never with pipes as truly blown
They pipe us yet where birds are flying
Beyond the ridge to lands unknown
Where we, once come, could boast when dying
We had not always lived alone.

II

When the indefinable
Moment apprises
Man of Its presence,
Shorn of disguises
Himself in his essence
Combines and comprises
The uncombinable.

With cabbage-whites white
And blue sky blue
And the world made one
Since two make two,
This moment only
Yet eras through
He walks in the sun
No longer lonely.

When the unobtainable
Seeming-disdaining
Vision is captured,
Beyond explaining
He can but, enraptured,
Accept this regaining
The unregainable.

With straws in the wind
And stars in the head
And the grail next door,
Though the wind drop dead
And the thresholded sentry
Forbid — let him tread
By the light in his core,
He still finds entry.

When the undreamable
Dream comes clearer

And all things distant
Newer and nearer,
All things existent
Grow suddenly dearer —
Wholly redeemable.

IV

Man woman and child
Being each unique
(Their strength and weakness)
Yet some to some
Who glance or speak
Would seem to come
Having more uniqueness;
Come less defiled
Whether strong or weak;
Come more unique
Man woman or child.

King queen and clown
Having each his day
For fame or laughter,
Yet some who came
That selfsame way
Seem never the same
As those came after
Or lost their crown
Before them. They
Keep each their day,
King queen and clown.

Live man and dead
Being each unique
(Their pain and glory),
Yet some will have left
By force or freak
To us the bereft

Some richer story;
Their say being said,
They still can speak
Words more unique,
More live, less dead.

VI

The gull hundreds of miles below him —
    Was it the Muse?
The cloud thousands of miles above him —
    Was it the Muse?
The river intoning his saga over and over,
The siren blaring her long farewell to Dover,
The grasshopper snipping scissors in the clover —
    Were they the Muse or no?

So those who carry this birthright and this burden
Regardless of all else must always listen
On the odd chance some fact or freak or phantom
Might tell them what they want, might burst the cordon
Which isolates them from their inmost vision.

The cradle thousands of years behind him —
    Was it the Muse?
The coffin a headstone's throw before him —
    Is it the Muse?
The clock that is ever impeding, ever abetting,
The bed that is ever remembering, ever forgetting,
The sun ever rising and setting, unrising, unsetting —
    Are they the Muse or no?

So those endowed with such a doom and heirloom
When others can be carefree must be careful
(Though sometimes, when the rest are careful, carefree),
Must wait for the unimmediately apparent
And grasp the Immediate — fairly or unfairly.

The world one millimetre beyond him --
   Is it the Muse?
The soul untold light years inside him —
   Is it the Muse?
The python of the past with coils unending,
The lion of the present roaring, rending,
The grey dove of the future still descending —
   Are they the Muse? Or no?

Invocation

Dolphin plunge, fountain play.
Fetch me far and far away.

Fetch me far my nursery toys,
Fetch me far my mother's hand,
Fetch me far the painted joys.

And when the painted cock shall crow
Fetch me far my waking day
That I may dance before I go.

Fetch me far the breeze in the heat,
Fetch me far the curl of the wave,
Fetch me far the face in the street.

And when the other faces throng
Fetch me far a place in the mind
Where only truthful things belong.

Fetch me far a moon in a tree,
Fetch me far a phrase of the wind,
Fetch me far the verb To Be.

And when the last horn burns the hills
Fetch me far one draught of grace
To quench my thirst before it kills.

Dolphin plunge, fountain play.
Fetch me far and far away.

The Slow Starter

A watched clock never moves, they said:
Leave it alone and you'll grow up.
Nor will the sulking holiday train
Start sooner if you stamp your feet.
   He left the clock to go its way;
   The whistle blew, the train went gay.

Do not press me so, she said;
Leave me alone and I will write
But not just yet, I am sure you know
The problem. Do not count the days.
   He left the calendar alone;
   The postman knocked, no letter came.

O never force the pace, they said;
Leave it alone, you have lots of time,
Your kind of work is none the worse
For slow maturing. Do not rush.
   He took their tip, he took his time,
   And found his time and talent gone.

Oh you have had your chance, It said;
Left it alone and it was one.
Who said a watched clock never moves?
Look at it now. Your chance was I.
   He turned and saw the accusing clock
   Race like a torrent round a rock.

Dark Age Glosses

on the Venerable Bede

Birds flitting in and out of the barn
Bring back an Anglo-Saxon story:
The great wooden hall with long fires down the centre,
Their feet in the rushes, their hands tearing the meat.
Suddenly high above them they notice a swallow enter
From the black storm and zigzag over their heads,
Then out once more into the unknown night;
And that, someone remarks, is the life of man.
But now it is time to sleep; one by one
They rise from the bench and their gigantic shadows
Lurch on the shuddering walls. How can the world
Or the non-world beyond harbour a bird?
They close their eyes that smart from the woodsmoke: how
Can anyone even guess his whence and whither?
This indoors flying makes it seem absurd,
Although it itches and nags and flutters and yearns,
To postulate any other life than now.

on the Grettir Saga

The burly major they denied
The Victoria Cross because of his drinking habits,
Blown up soon after, for some reason reminds me
Of the strong man of Iceland who also died
Under the frown of the safe men, cooped in an islet
With a festering leg and a bad record:
An outrageous outlaw, his mind ill equipped,
His temper uncertain, too quick with his weapons,
Yet had done the scattered farms some service,
Also had made people laugh, like the major
Raising his elbow in the mess at 'Pindi;
But, unlike the major, Grettir was cursed,
Haunted by eyes in the dark, on his desolate
Rock on the fringe of the Arctic knew

The fear no man had ever induced in him,
And thus awaited his doom. Whereas
The major, who also was doomed, slept sound
And was merely cursed by the curse of his time.

on the Njal Saga

The tall blonde dabbing scent behind her ears
And throwing over her shoulder her Parthian curse
To leave her lover facing the world defenceless
Calls up the picture through one thousand years
Of a tall blonde with her hair to her waist, exulting
Over her husband with his bow-string cut
Because he had begged one strand of her hair to mend it.
'Yes indeed, my hair could save your life now — But
Do you remember that slap you gave me once?'
So Gunnar stood with the roof off over his head
And his enemies closed in. She watched and smiled.
Almost reluctantly they left him dead
And they and she thus left a legacy
Of many deaths to come — man, woman and child —
And one great saga casting from those dark
Ages a lighthouse ray, a reminder that even then,
For all the spite and hatred and betrayal,
Men had the nobler qualities of men.

on the Four Masters

The light was no doubt the same, the ecology different :
All Ireland drowned in woods. Those who today
Think it a golden age and at Glendalough
Or Clonmacnois let imagination play
Like flame upon those ruins should keep in mind
That the original actual flames were often
Kindled not by the Norsemen but by the monks'
Compatriots, boorish kings who, mad to find
Loot to outride each other's ambition, would stop
At nothing — which so often led to nothing.

Which is even — tell it not in the Gaelic League —
True of the High King Brian whose eighty years,
Caught in a web of largely his own intrigue,
Soured him with power and rusted him with blood
To let him die in a tent on a cold Good Friday
To earn his niche. And yet he earned his niche.
The last battle was his; maybe the sun came out
Before the defeated Norseman struck him, before
History endorsed the triumph and the rout.
The light was no doubt the same — and just as rich.

Nature Notes

Dandelions

Incorrigible, brash,
They brightened the cinder path of my childhood,
Unsubtle, the opposite of primroses,
But, unlike primroses, capable
Of growing anywhere, railway track, pierhead,
Like our extrovert friends who never
Make us fall in love, yet fill
The primroseless roseless gaps.

Cats

Incorrigible, uncommitted,
They leavened the long flat hours of my childhood,
Subtle, the opposite of dogs,
And, unlike dogs, capable
Of flirting, falling, and yawning anywhere,
Like women who want no contract
But going their own way
Make the way of their lovers lighter.

Corncrakes

Incorrigible, unmusical,
They bridged the surrounding hedge of my childhood,
Unsubtle, the opposite of blackbirds,
But, unlike blackbirds, capable
Anywhere they are of endorsing summer
Like loud men around the corner
Whom we never see but whose raucous
Voices can give us confidence.

Incorrigible, ruthless,
It rattled the shingly beach of my childhood,
Subtle, the opposite of earth,
And, unlike earth, capable
Any time at all of proclaiming eternity
Like something or someone to whom
We have to surrender, finding
Through that surrender life.

The Park

Through a glass greenly men as trees walking
Led by their dogs, trees as torrents
Loosed by the thaw, tulips as shriekmarks
(Yelps of delight), lovers as coracles
Riding the rapids: Spring as a spring
Releasing the jack-in-a-box of a fanfare.

Urban enclave of lawns and water,
Lacquered ducks and young men sculling,
Children who never had seen the country
Believing it this while those who had once
Known real country ignore the void
Their present imposes, their past exposes.

South and east lie the yellowed terraces
Grandiose, jerrybuilt, ghosts of gracious
Living, and north those different terraces
Where great white bears with extensile necks,
Convicted sentries, lope their beat,
No rest for their paws till the day they die.

Fossils of flesh, fossils of stucco:
Between them the carefully labelled flower beds
And the litter baskets, but also between them
Through a grill gaily men as music
Forcing the spring to loose the lid,
To break the bars, to find the world.

The Lake in the Park

On an empty morning a small clerk
Who thinks no one will ever love him
Sculls on the lake in the park while bosomy
Trees indifferently droop above him.

On the bank a father and mother goose
Hiss as he passes, pigeons are courting,
Everything mocks; the empty deck-chairs
Are set in pairs, there is no consorting

For him with nature or man, the ducks
Go arrowheading across his bows
Adding insult to absence, his mood
Disallows what the sun endows.

The water arrows are barbed; their barbs,
Corrugated like flint, can start
No Stone Age echoes in his mind
And yet they too might pierce his heart.

Dogs in the Park

The precise yet furtive etiquette of dogs
Makes them ignore the whistle while they talk
In circles round each other, one-man bonds
Deferred in pauses of this man-made walk
To open vistas to a past of packs

That raven round the stuccoed terraces
And scavenge at the mouth of Stone Age caves;
What man proposes dog on his day disposes
In litter round both human and canine graves,
Then lifts his leg to wash the gravestones clean,

While simultaneously his eyes express
Apology and contempt; his master calls
And at the last and sidelong he returns,
Part heretic, part hack, and jumps and crawls
And fumbles to communicate and fails.

And then they leave the park, the leads are snapped
On to the spiky collars, the tails wag
For no known reason and the ears are pricked
To search through legendary copse and crag
For legendary creatures doomed to die
Even as they, the dogs, were doomed to live.

Sunday in the Park

No sunlight ever. Bleak trees whisper ironies,
Carolina duck and Canada goose forget
Their world across the water, red geraniums
Enhance the chill, dark glasses mirror ironies,
The prams are big with doom, the walkers-out forget
Why they are out, London is lost, geraniums
Stick it out in the wind, old men feel lost
But stick it out and refugees forget
Pretences and grow sad while ironies
Frill out from sprinklers on the green veneer
That screens the tubes in which congested trains
Get stuck like enemas or ironies
Half lost between the lines while dachshunds run
Like centipedes and no one knows the time
Whatever foreigners ask it. Here is Sunday:
And on the seventh day He rested. The Tree
Forgets both good and evil in irony.

Jungle Clearance Ceylon

In a manmade lake at first light
Cruising between the tops of bleached
Skeleton trees we waited for elephant
Coming to drink. They never came
But, focussing in, on each bare branch
Of the bonewhite trees we marked a pelican
Frozen to fossil, looking down
Its beak in contempt of human beings
Who had drowned a valley to found a town —
Power and water for human beings
In the thick of the bush. In the thin of the trees
The pelican perched as though in a glass
Case where the wind could never blow
Nor elephant come to drink nor human
Beings presume in the grey dawn
To press a button or throw a switch
To slap the west on the back of the east
In spite of archaic and absent elephant
In spite of archaic and present pelican
In spite of themselves as human beings.

Vistas

Emerging from aeons of ocean on to the shore
The creature found itself in a roadless
Forest where nothing stretched before
Its lack of limbs but lack of hope
Until the trees, millennia later,
Parted to grant it greater scope.

Emerging from miles of tunnel into a plain
The train finds itself in a foreign
Beatitude. Creeping fog and rain
And deafmute fears are left behind;
The stuttering grub grows wings and sings
The tune it never thought to find.

Emerging from years of lacking into a love
The Self finds itself in predestined
Freedom. Around, below, above,
Glinting fish and piping birds
Deny that earth and truth are only
Earth, respectively, and words.

Reflections

The mirror above my fireplace reflects the reflected
Room in my windows; I look in the mirror at night
And see two rooms, the first where left is right
And the second, beyond the reflected window, corrected
But there I am standing back to my back. The standard
Lamp comes thrice in my mirror, twice in my window,
The fire in the mirror lies two rooms away through the window,
The fire in the window lies one room away down the terrace,
My actual room stands sandwiched between confections
Of night and lights and glass and in both directions
I can see beyond and through the reflections the street lamps
At home outdoors where my indoors rooms lie stranded,
Where a taxi perhaps will drive in through the bookcase
Whose books are not for reading and past the fire
Which gives no warmth and pull up by my desk
At which I cannot write since I am not lefthanded.

Hold-Up

The lights were red, refused to change,
Ash-ends grew longer, no one spoke,
The papers faded in their hands,
The bubbles in the football pools
Went flat, the hot news froze, the dates
They could not keep were dropped like charred
Matches, the girls no longer flagged
Their sex, besides the code was lost,
The engine stalled, a tall glass box
On the pavement held a corpse in pickle
His ear still cocked, and no one spoke,
No number rang, for miles behind
The other buses nudged and blared
And no one dared get out. The conductress
Was dark and lost, refused to change.

The Wiper

Through purblind night the wiper
Reaps a swathe of water
On the screen; we shudder on
    And hardly hold the road,
All we can see a segment
Of blackly shining asphalt
With the wiper moving across it
    Clearing, blurring, clearing.

But what to say of the road?
The monotony of its hardly
Visible camber, the mystery
    Of its far invisible margins,
Will these be always with us,
The night being broken only
By lights that pass or meet us
    From others in moving boxes?

Boxes of glass and water,
Upholstered, equipped with dials
Professing to tell the distance
    We have gone, the speed we are going,
But never a gauge nor needle
To tell us where we are going
Or when day will come, supposing
    This road exists in daytime.

For now we cannot remember
Where we were when it was not
Night, when it was not raining,
    Before this car moved forward
And the wiper backward and forward
Lighting so little before us
Of a road that, crouching forward,
    We watch move always towards us,

Which through the tiny segment
Cleared and blurred by the wiper
Is sucked in under the axle
    To be spewed behind us and lost
While we, dazzled by darkness,
Haul the black future towards us
Peeling the skin from our hands;
    And yet we hold the road.

The Blasphemies

The sin against the Holy . . . though what
He wondered was it? Cold in his bed
He thought: If I think those words I know
Yet must not be thinking — Come to the hurdle
And I shall be damned through thinking Damn —
But Whom? But no! Those words are unthinkable;
Damn anyone else, but once I — No,
Here lies the unforgivable blasphemy.
So pulling the cold sheets over his head
He swore to himself he had not thought
Those words he knew but never admitted.
To be damned at seven years old was early.

Ten years later, his Who's Who
No longer cosmic, he turned to parody —
Prayers, hymns, the Apostles' Creed —
Preening himself as a gay blasphemer,
But what is a practical joke in a world
Of nonsense, what is a rational attitude
Towards politics in a world of cyphers,
Towards sex if you lack all lust, towards art
If you do not believe in communication?
And what is a joke about God if you do not
Accept His existence? Where is the blasphemy?
No Hell at seventeen feels empty.

Rising thirty, he had decided
God was a mere expletive, a cheap one,
No longer worth a laugh, no longer
A proper occasion to prove one's freedom
By denying something not worth denying.
So humanism was all and the only
Sin was the sin against the Human —
But you could not call it Ghost for that

Was merely emotive; the only — you could not
Call it sin for that was emotive —
The only failure was not to face
The facts. But at thirty what are the facts?

Ten years later, in need of myth,
He thought: I can use my childhood symbols
Divorced from their context, Manger and Cross
Could do very well for Tom Dick and Harry —
Have we not all of us been in a war
So have we not carried call it a cross
Which was never our fault? Yet how can a cross
Be never your fault? The words of the myth,
Now merely that and no longer faith,
Melt in his hands which were never proved
Hard as nails, nor can he longer
Speak for the world — or himself — at forty.

Forty to fifty. In ten years
He grew to feel the issue irrelevant:
Tom Dick and Harry were not Christ
And whether Christ were God or not
And whether there were a God or not
The word was inadequate. For himself
He was not Tom or Dick or Harry,
Let alone God, he was merely fifty,
No one and nowhere else, a walking
Question but no more cheap than any
Question or quest is cheap. The sin
Against the Holy Ghost — What is it?

Selva Oscura

A house can be haunted by those who were never there
If there was where they were missed. Returning to such
Is it worse if you miss the same or another or none?
The haunting anyway is too much.
You have to leave the house to clear the air.

A life can be haunted by what it never was
If that were merely glimpsed. Lost in the maze
That means yourself and never out of the wood
These days, though lost, will be all your days;
Life, if you leave it, must be left for good.

And yet for good can be also where I am,
Stumbling among dark treetrunks, should I meet
One sudden shaft of light from the hidden sky
Or, finding bluebells bathe my feet,
Know that the world, though more, is also I.

Perhaps suddenly too I strike a clearing and see
Some unknown house — or was it mine? — but now
It welcomes whom I miss in welcoming me;
The door swings open and a hand
Beckons to all the life my days allow.

Soap Suds

This brand of soap has the same smell as once in the big
House he visited when he was eight: the walls of the bathroom
    open
To reveal a lawn where a great yellow ball rolls back through a
    hoop
To rest at the head of a mallet held in the hands of a child.

And these were the joys of that house: a tower with a telescope;
Two great faded globes, one of the earth, one of the stars;
A stuffed black dog in the hall; a walled garden with bees;
A rabbit warren; a rockery; a vine under glass; the sea.

To which he has now returned. The day of course is fine
And a grown-up voice cries Play! The mallet slowly swings,
Then crack, a great gong booms from the dog-dark hall and the
    ball
Skims forward through the hoop and then through the next and
    then

Through hoops where no hoops were and each dissolves in turn
And the grass has grown head-high and an angry voice cries Play!
But the ball is lost and the mallet slipped long since from the hands
Under the running tap that are not the hands of a child.

The Suicide

And this, ladies and gentlemen, whom I am not in fact
Conducting, was his office all those minutes ago,
This man you never heard of. There are the bills
In the intray, the ash in the ashtray, the grey memoranda stacked
Against him, the serried ranks of the box-files, the packed
Jury of his unanswered correspondence
Nodding under the paperweight in the breeze
From the window by which he left; and here is the cracked
Receiver that never got mended and here is the jotter
With his last doodle which might be his own digestive tract
Ulcer and all or might be the flowery maze
Through which he had wandered deliciously till he stumbled
Suddenly finally conscious of all he lacked
On a manhole under the hollyhocks. The pencil
Point had obviously broken, yet, when he left his room
By catdrop sleight-of-foot or simple vanishing act,
To those who knew him for all that mess in the street
This man with the shy smile has left behind
Something that was intact.

Pet Shop

Cold blood or warm, crawling or fluttering
Bric-à-brac, all are here to be bought,
Noisy or silent, python or myna,
Fish with long silk trains like dowagers,
Monkeys lost to thought.

In a small tank tiny enamelled
Green terrapin jostle, in a cage a crowd
Of small birds elbow each other and bicker
While beyond the ferrets, eardrum, eyeball
Find that macaw too loud.

Here behind glass lies a miniature desert,
The sand littered with rumpled gauze
Discarded by snakes like used bandages;
In the next door desert fossilized lizards
Stand in a pose, a pause.

But most of the customers want something comfy —
Rabbit, hamster, potto, puss —
Something to hold on the lap and cuddle
Making believe it will return affection
Like some neutered succubus.

Purr then or chirp, you are here for our pleasure,
Here at the mercy of our whim and purse;
Once there was the wild, now tanks and cages,
But we can offer you a home, a haven,
That might prove even worse.

Flower Show

Marooned by night in a canvas cathedral under bare bulbs
He plods the endless aisles not daring to close an eye
To massed brass bands of flowers; these flowers are not to pluck
Which (cream cheese, paper, glass, all manner of textile and
    plastic)
Having long since forgotten, if they ever knew, the sky
Are grown, being forced, uprooted.

Squidlike, phallic or vulvar, hypnotic, idiotic, oleaginous,
Fanged or whaleboned, wattled or balding, brimstone or cold
As trout or seaweed, these blooms, ogling or baneful, all
Keep him in their blind sights; he tries to stare them down
But they are too many, too unreal, their aims are one, the controlled
Aim of a firing party.

So bandage his eyes since he paid to come in but somehow forgot
To follow the others out — and now there is no way out
Except that his inturned eyes before he falls may show him
Some-nettled orchard, tousled hedge, some garden even
Where flowers, whether they boast or insinuate, whisper or shout,
Still speak a living language.

The Taxis

In the first taxi he was alone tra-la,
No extras on the clock. He tipped ninepence
But the cabby, while he thanked him, looked askance
As though to suggest someone had bummed a ride.

In the second taxi he was alone tra-la
But the clock showed sixpence extra; he tipped according
And the cabby from out of his muffler said: 'Make sure
You have left nothing behind tra-la between you'.

In the third taxi he was alone tra-la
But the tip-up seats were down and there was an extra
Charge of one-and-sixpence and an odd
Scent that reminded him of a trip to Cannes.

As for the fourth taxi, he was alone
Tra-la when he hailed it but the cabby looked
Through him and said: 'I can't tra-la well take
So many people, not to speak of the dog.'

After the Crash

When he came to he knew
Time must have passed because
The asphalt was high with hemlock
Through which he crawled to his crash
Helmet and found it no more
Than his wrinkled hand what it was.

Yet life seemed still going on:
He could hear the signals bounce
Back from the moon and the hens
Fire themselves black in the batteries
And the silence of small blind cats
Debating whether to pounce.

Then he looked up and marked
The gigantic scales in the sky,
The pan on the left dead empty
And the pan on the right dead empty,
And knew in the dead, dead calm
It was too late to die.

Another Cold May

With heads like chessmen, bishop or queen,
The tulips tug at their roots and mourn
In inaudible frequencies, the move
Is the wind's, not theirs; fender to fender
The cars will never emerge, not even
Should their owners emerge to claim them, the move
Is time's, not theirs; elbow to elbow
Inside the roadhouse drinks are raised
And downed, and downed, the pawns and drains
Are blocked, are choked, the move is nil,
The lounge is, like the carpark, full,
The tulips also feel the chill
And tilting leeward do no more
Than mimic a bishop's move, the square
Ahead remains ahead, their petals
Will merely fall and choke the drains
Which will be all; this month remains
False animation of failed levitation,
The move is time's, the loss is ours.

Ravenna

What do I remember of my visit to Ravenna? Firstly,
That I had come from Venice where I had come from Greece
So that my eyes seemed dim and the world flat. Secondly,
That after Tintoretto's illusory depth and light
The mosaics knocked me flat. There they stood. The geese
Had hissed as they pecked the corn from Theodora's groin,
Yet here she stands on the wall of San Vitale, as bright
As life and a long shot taller, self-made empress,
Who patronised the monophysites and the Greens
And could have people impaled. There was also and thirdly the
    long
Lost naval port of Caesar, surviving now in the name
In Classe: the sea today is behind the scenes
Like his Liburnian galleys. What went wrong
With Byzantium as with Rome went slowly, their fame
Sunk in malarial marsh. The flat lands now
Are ruled by a sugar refinery and a church,
Sant' Apollinare in Classe. What do I remember of Ravenna?
A bad smell mixed with glory, and the cold
Eyes that belie the tessellated gold.

Charon

The conductor's hands were black with money:
Hold on to your ticket, he said, the inspector's
Mind is black with suspicion, and hold on to
That dissolving map. We moved through London,
We could see the pigeons through the glass but failed
To hear their rumours of wars, we could see
The lost dog barking but never knew
That his bark was as shrill as a cock crowing,
We just jogged on, at each request
Stop there was a crowd of aggressively vacant
Faces, we just jogged on, eternity
Gave itself airs in revolving lights
And then we came to the Thames and all
The bridges were down, the further shore
Was lost in fog, so we asked the conductor
What we should do. He said: Take the ferry
Faute de mieux. We flicked the flashlight
And there was the ferryman just as Virgil
And Dante had seen him. He looked at us coldly
And his eyes were dead and his hands on the oar
Were black with obols and varicose veins
Marbled his calves and he said to us coldly:
If you want to die you will have to pay for it.

The Introduction

They were introduced in a grave glade
And she frightened him because she was young
And thus too late. Crawly crawly
Went the twigs above their heads and beneath
The grass beneath their feet the larvae
Split themselves laughing. Crawly crawly
Went the cloud above the treetops reaching
For a sun that lacked the nerve to set
And he frightened her because he was old
And thus too early. Crawly crawly
Went the string quartet that was tuning up
In the back of the mind. You two should have met
Long since, he said, or else not now.
The string quartet in the back of the mind
Was all tuned up with nowhere to go.
They were introduced in a green grave.

The Habits

When they put him in rompers the habits
Fanned out to close in, they were dressed
In primary colours and each of them
Carried a rattle and a hypodermic;
His parents said it was all for the best.

Next, the barracks of boys: the habits
Slapped him on the back, they were dressed
In pinstripe trousers and carried
A cheque book, a passport, and a sjambok;
The master said it was all for the best.

And then came the woman: the habits
Pretended to leave, they were dressed
In bittersweet undertones and carried
A Parthian shaft and an affidavit;
The adgirl said it was all for the best.

Age became middle: the habits
Made themselves at home, they were dressed
In quilted dressing-gowns and carried
A decanter, a siphon, and a tranquilliser;
The computer said it was all for the best.

Then age became real: the habits
Outstayed their welcome, they were dressed
In nothing and carried nothing.
He said: If you won't go, I go.
The Lord God said it was all for the best.

Greyness is All

If black were truly black not grey
It might provide some depth to pray
Against and we could hope that white
Would reach a corresponding height.

But, as it is, we melt and droop
Within the confines of our coop;
The mind stays grey, obtuse, inert,
And grey the feathers in the dirt.

If only some black demon would
Infuse our small grey souls we could
At least attempt to break the wire
That bounds the Gadarene hens' desire.

But, as it is, we needs must wait
Not for some demon but some fate
Contrived by men and never known
Until the final switch is thrown

To black out all the worlds of men
And demons too but even then
Whether that black will not prove grey
No one may wait around to say.

from *Memoranda to Horace*

II

Returned from my far-near country, my erstwhile,
I wonder how much we are defined by negatives,
  Who have no more seen the Bandusian
Spring than have you the unreadable Atlantic,

You to whom seraph and gargoyle were meaningless
And I to whom Roman roads are a tedium
  Preferring the boreens of a country
Rome never bothered her ponderous head about.

So what have we, Flaccus, in common? If I never
Boasted a Maecenas, you never summarised
  Life from Rockefeller Centre
And if you never moved in a Christian framework

I never moved in a pagan; for that matter
I no more found Tir na nÓg than you
  The Hesperides, yet vice versa
If you never found Tir na nÓg, then I never

Found the Hesperides. It looks as if both of us
Met in the uniqueness of history a premise
  That keeps us apart yet parallel,
The gap reducible only by language.

It is noisy today as it was when Brutus
Fell on his sword, yet through wars and rumours
  Of wars I would pitch on the offchance
My voice to reach you. Yours had already

Crossed the same gap to the north and future,
Offering no consolation, simply
  Telling me how you had gathered
Your day, a choice it is mine to emulate.

III

'Or with the tangles' as one of our own said
And another called it 'intense' but admiringly 'levity',
   This in the Nineteen-Thirties
Had you, Flaccus, been alive and improbably
   Tempted by the Party would as usual
      Have served as a second string.

Yes, Augustus had to arrive in a sealed train
And you had to praise him and even think you meant it
   The way you meant it for Regulus;
Yet we can guess between politics and personal
   Ties what making your expected
      Bow you really preferred,

Slipping away to Lalage. There in the shade
Of an ilex you could forget the triumphal arches
   And the rigged votes; the repetitive
Cicadas endorsed your sleep after lovemaking
   From which deliciously laughing
      She woke and gave you a phrase,

Which you dressed out in nonsense, that old yarn
Of the routed wolf, and yet today in London
   When all the loudspeakers bellow
'Wolf repeat Wolf!' I can find asylum,
   As you did, either in language
      Or laughter or with the tangles.

IV

Though elderly poets profess to be inveterate
Dionysians, despising Apollonians,
   I find it, Flaccus, more modest
To attempt, like you, an appetitive decorum.

Contraptions in ear or mouth or vagina,
To you known neither as aid nor indignity,
     Assist yet degrade a generation
For whom quality has long been in pawn to security.

Which you, though they called you a time-serving parasite,
Must understand, though even your period
     Never foresaw such appalling
Stress upon mere irredeemable quantity.

So now, when faced by a too well evacuated
Sanatorium or mildewed junkshop,
     The point is never to recognize
Any preconception : let commonplace be novelty.

Which you, had they called you a legacy hunter,
Would yet have agreed, no matter how the market
     Jittered : the point was to recognize
The unborn face and the nigger in the woodpile.

Both of which gifts, whether non-recognition
Or pre-recognition, can serve us two thousand
     Years after yours as an antidote
To the poison of time and manoeuvre a compromise

With horrible old fellows, glazed and jowly,
Who were the ones we always avoided
     Yet soon to be resembled albeit
Our juniors resemble ourselves in avoidance.

Coda

Maybe we knew each other better
When the night was young and unrepeated
And the moon stood still over Jericho.

So much for the past; in the present
There are moments caught between heart-beats
When maybe we know each other better.

But what is that clinking in the darkness?
Maybe we shall know each other better
When the tunnels meet beneath the mountain.

TRANSLATIONS

from *The Agamemnon of Aeschylus*

O Zeus our king and Night our friend
Donor of glories,
Night who cast on the towers of Troy
A close-clinging net so that neither the grown
Nor any of the children can pass
The enslaving and huge
Trap of all-taking destruction.
Great Zeus, guardian of host and guest,
I honour who has done his work and taken
A leisured aim at Paris so that neither
Too short nor yet over the stars
   He might shoot to no purpose.

From Zeus is the blow they can tell of,
This at least can be established,
They have fared according to his ruling. For some
Deny that the gods deign to consider those among men
Who trample on the grace of inviolate things;
It is the impious man says this,
For Ruin is revealed the child
Of not to be attempted actions
When men are puffed up unduly
And their houses are stuffed with riches.
Measure is the best. Let danger be distant,
This should suffice a man
With a proper part of wisdom.
   For a man has no protection
   Against the drunkenness of riches
   Once he has spurned from his sight
   The high altar of Justice.

Sombre Persuasion compels him,
Intolerable child of calculating Doom;
All cure is vain, there is no glozing it over
But the mischief shines forth with a deadly light
And like bad coinage
By rubbings and frictions
He stands discoloured and black
Under the test — like a boy
Who chases a winged bird
He has branded his city for ever.
His prayers are heard by no god;
Who makes such things his practice
The gods destroy him.
　　This way came Paris
　　To the house of the sons of Atreus
　　And outraged the table of friendship
　　Stealing the wife of his host.

Leaving to her countrymen clanging of
Shields and of spears and
Launching of warships
And bringing instead of a dowry destruction to Troy
Lightly she was gone through the gates daring
Things undared. Many the groans
Of the palace spokesmen on this theme —
'O the house, the house, and its princes,
O the bed and the imprint of her limbs;
One can see him crouching in silence
Dishonoured and unreviling.'
Through desire for her who is overseas, a ghost
Will seem to rule the household.
　　And now her husband hates
　　The grace of shapely statues;
　　In the emptiness of their eyes
　　All their appeal is departed.

But appearing in dreams persuasive
Images come bringing a joy that is vain,

Vain for when in fancy he looks to touch her —
Slipping through his hands the vision
Rapidly is gone
Following on wings the walks of sleep.
Such are his griefs in his house on his hearth,
Such as these and worse than these,
But everywhere through the land of Greece which men have left
Are mourning women with enduring hearts
To be seen in all houses; many
Are the thoughts which stab their hearts:
    For those they sent to war
    They know, but in place of men
    That which comes home to them
    Is merely an urn and ashes.

But the money-changer War, changer of bodies,
Holding his balance in the battle
Home from Troy refined by fire
Sends back to friends the dust
That is heavy with tears, stowing
A man's worth of ashes
In an easily handled jar.
And they wail speaking well of the men how that one
Was expert in battle, and one fell well in the carnage —
But for another man's wife.
Muffled and muttered words;
And resentful grief creeps up against the sons
Of Atreus and their cause.
    But others there by the wall
    Entombed in Trojan ground
    Lie, handsome of limb,
    Holding and hidden in enemy soil.

Heavy is the murmur of an angry people
Performing the purpose of a public curse;
There is something cowled in the night
That I anxiously wait to hear.
For the gods are not blind to the

Murderers of many and the black
Furies in time
When a man prospers in sin
By erosion of life reduce him to darkness,
Who, once among the lost, can no more
Be helped. Over-great glory
Is a sore burden. The high peak
Is blasted by the eyes of Zeus.

 I prefer an unenvied fortune,
 Not to be a sacker of cities
 Nor to find myself living at another's
 Ruling, myself a captive.

 · · · · · · ·

CLYTEMNESTRA

There is the sea and who shall drain it dry? It breeds
Its wealth in silver of plenty of purple gushing
And ever-renewed, the dyeings of our garments.
The house has its store of these by God's grace, King.
This house is ignorant of poverty
And I would have vowed a pavement of many garments
Had the palace oracle enjoined that vow
Thereby to contrive a ransom for his life.
For while there is root, foliage comes to the house
Spreading a tent of shade against the Dog Star.
So now that you have reached your hearth and home
You prove a miracle — advent of warmth in winter ;
And further this — even in the time of heat
When God is fermenting wine from the bitter grape,
Even then it is cool in the house if only
Its master walk at home, a grown man, ripe.
O Zeus the Ripener, ripen these my prayers ;
Your part it is to make the ripe fruit fall.

Solvitur Acris Hiems

(HORACE, *Odes*, I. 4)

Winter to Spring: the west wind melts the frozen rancour,
    The windlass drags to sea the thirsty hull;
Byre is no longer welcome to beast or fire to ploughman,
    The field removes the frost-cap from his skull.

Venus of Cythera leads the dances under the hanging
    Moon and the linked line of Nymphs and Graces
Beat the ground with measured feet while the busy Fire-God
    Stokes his red-hot mills in volcanic places.

Now is the time to twine the spruce and shining head with myrtle,
    Now with flowers escaped the earthy fetter,
And sacrifice to the woodland god in shady copses
    A lamb or a kid, whichever he likes better.

Equally heavy is the heel of white-faced Death on the pauper's
    Shack and the towers of kings, and O my dear
The little sum of life forbids the ravelling of lengthy
    Hopes. Night and the fabled dead are near

And the narrow house of nothing past whose lintel
    You will meet no wine like this, no boy to admire
Like Lycidas who today makes all young men a furnace
    And whom tomorrow girls will find a fire.